THE CASE OF THE
WANDERING WEATHERVANES

By the Same Author

The Case of the Wandering Weathervanes

A McGurk Mystery

BY E. W. HILDICK

Illustrated by Denise Brunkus

MACMILLAN PUBLISHING COMPANY
New York

Macmillan Publishing Company
866 Third Avenue, New York, NY 10022
Collier Macmillan Canada, Inc.
First Edition
Printed in the United States of America

10   9   8   7   6   5   4   3   2   1

The text of this book is set in 12 point Caledonia.
The illustrations are rendered in pencil.

Library of Congress Cataloging-in-Publication Data
Hildick, E. W. (Edmund Wallace), date.
The case of the wandering weathervanes.
Summary: McGurk's detectives begin to investigate
the thefts of numerous weathervanes and find themselves
tracking an enemy agent.
1. Mystery and detective stories.   I. Brunkus, Denise,
ill. II. Title.
PZ7.H5463Cavo   1988   [Fic]   87-13171
ISBN 0-02-743970-4

CONTENTS

1 Brains Reports a Crime

"Hey! I've been robbed!" said Brains Bellingham, as he burst into the McGurk basement that Saturday morning. His eyes were staring behind his big round glasses. He was flushed to the roots of his short, bristly hair. He was sweating. He must have run all the way. And he was *still* ten minutes late.

McGurk looked at him sourly. We were all sitting around the table, with McGurk at the head in his rocking chair. He'd already gotten into his stride, explaining why he'd called this extra-special meeting.

"International terrorism, men," he'd announced. "We at the McGurk Organization ought to be prepared to tackle it."

International terrorism!

I was wondering how it could ever in a million years have anything to do with *our* neighborhood.

Even Willie Sandowsky looked doubtful.

"You mean—like hijacking planes, McGurk?" he said, rubbing his long, thin nose.

"Maybe he's thinking someone might hijack the school bus, Willie," said Wanda Grieg, giving her long, blond hair a scornful toss.

"Or plant bombs outside the Town Hall, Chief McGurk?" said Mari Yoshimura, looking grave, but with a sparkle in her dark eyes.

"You never know!" growled McGurk. "And it's no laughing matter, Officer Grieg!"

"I wasn't—" Wanda began.

Which was when Brains burst in.

McGurk's green eyes widened, but only to give our science expert a cold stare. Even his fiery red hair did nothing to warm up his expression.

"*You*—have been—*robbed*?" he said.

We others stirred uneasily, but Brains didn't flinch.

He glared right back. "Yeah! I *have* been robbed!"

McGurk glanced around at us with a faint smirk that seemed to say, Just watch me take him apart!

"Did someone borrow your bike without permission, Officer Bellingham?" he said. "Is that it?"

"Your bike which you left *unlocked*?" said Wanda, piling it on.

Brains shook his head.

"Of course not! Would I be so dumb as to do that?"

"Yes," said Wanda.

"Be quiet!" snapped McGurk, who doesn't like to be interrupted, especially when conducting his disciplinary hearings. He turned to Brains. "So if it wasn't your bike, what then?"

Brains was still glaring, but there were tears in his eyes now.

"Was it your trick-or-treat bag?" asked Willie, full of sympathy.

(We'd had an excellent Halloween the evening before, with myself, Wanda, Willie, Brains, and Mari dressed as old-time escaped convicts, chained together, and Guess Who as the triumphant Deputy Sheriff leading us back to jail.)

Brains shook his head, gulped, and said, "Worse than that, Willie! Much worse!"

Mari gasped.

"Oh, dear! Not your McGurk Organization ID card?"

This time there was no twinkle in her eyes. She is the newest member and she'd had to work very hard to get her own ID card.

Even McGurk looked very tense then. No regular cop who'd allowed someone to steal his badge and gun could have been in greater danger of immediate suspension than Brains was at that moment.

Brains opened his mouth to say something, but became choked up.

Now we were all getting tense.

Being the Organization's record keeper, there was only one thing *I* would have found so upsetting.

"Hey, Brains!" I said. "Don't tell me they stole your *notes*?"

He looked at me. "Notes?" he said, in a croaky whisper.

"Yes. The notes for some science thing you were working on? Some new invention?"

That produced results.

"Worse, Joey!" he said. "They stole the prototype itself!"

Mari gasped again. Her father owns electronics factories. I reckon he must spend hundreds of thousands of dollars guarding the prototypes of *his* new products.

"Prototype of *what*, for pete's sake?" said McGurk.

"The thing I've been working on," said Brains. "My new special electronic-linked weathervane."

"It's the first *I've* heard of it," said Wanda.

"That's because I haven't perfected it yet," said Brains. "But I was—was getting close," he added, fighting back a sob.

"Tell us more," said McGurk.

There was no sympathy in *his* voice. Just professional interest. I guess he'd decided that although this was nowhere near as spectacular as terrorism, it did have a kind of international big-time ring: the stealing of plans and prototypes for some new invention.

"And first," he added, "tell us what's so special about it."

"I just did," said Brains. "It has electrical connections to a panel that lights up, so you can see even in the dark which way the wind is blowing, and how strong."

"So they took the weathervane and panel and—"

"Oh, no!" said Brains. "Just the vane. I had it mounted on the garage roof. It . . ."

His voice trailed off. McGurk was looking mad again. If Brains had been working on a new missile launcher or something like that, McGurk might have stayed interested. But this—no.

"Penny-ante stuff!" he snorted.

I had to agree.

"Yeah! You told us it was the prototype of your

new invention, Brains. Well, it seems to me that the vane is only *part* of it."

"I bet it's just some kid's prank, anyway," said Wanda.

"Oh, yeah?" said Brains. "Well, if it is, it's a pretty *expensive* prank! Because mine isn't the only weathervane that's been swiped. There are two others missing on our street, and one of them is worth over two hundred dollars. And Mrs. Getzoff said they'd stolen one on East Elm worth three *thousand!*"

There was a scraping sound. McGurk's chair. Being pushed back.

"Well, why didn't you say so at first, Officer Bellingham?" He got to his feet. "We'll talk about international terrorism some other time, men. This sounds worth looking into." He began to put on his coat. "It's still a prank, probably, but you never know. Lots of major crimes start out as pranks, after all."

"Even penny-ante pranks, McGurk?" said Wanda.

"Even penny-ante pranks, Officer Grieg," said McGurk. "Besides, even if that's all it is, it'll be good practice. Let's see if we can't crack it wide open by lunchtime."

"Lunchtime, McGurk?" said Brains. "But it's ten-thirty already!"

McGurk shrugged.

"Well, by nightfall, then. Because if it *is* a prank"—he looked hard at Wanda—"I have a pretty good idea who the perpetrator might be."

Wanda blushed. We all knew what McGurk was driving at. Wanda's brother, Ed, is one of the biggest practical jokers in the whole town.

"Anyway, let's go get more details," said McGurk. "Starting with the scene of the crime."

2 The Scene of the Crime

The spindle looked very forlorn on the end of the Bellingham garage roof, with its crude letters *N*, *E*, *S*, and *W* made from bent coathanger wire around its base.

"That's where the weathervane was mounted," said Brains.

"So all they had to do was *lift* it off the spike thing, huh?" said McGurk.

"Yes," said Brains. "In fact, that's all that's necessary with most weathervanes." He sighed. "Except with mine there were some wires they had to break off. On account of the electronic circuit, which is what makes mine so special."

"Yeah, yeah!" McGurk was thoughtfully eyeing the spindle. "It isn't very high, is it?"

"I know," said Brains. "A weathervane should really be fixed at the highest point around. But Mom wouldn't let me put it on the roof of the house and—"

"I should think *not!*" said Wanda. "Even I wouldn't want to go climbing up there!"

"And besides, it was only in the experimental stage," said Brains. "I wanted to have it handy while I made adjustments. I—"

"Officer Bellingham! We're here to investigate a crime. The reason I said it wasn't very high was to point out how easy it would be for the perpetrators to reach."

"Correct, Chief McGurk!" said Mari. "Even for a child."

"Just a short ladder," I said. "That's all it would take."

"Was there one lying around handy?" asked McGurk.

"No way!" said Brains. "The only steps here are in the garage. Which we keep locked at night."

"They wouldn't need steps, anyway," said Wanda. "All they'd need would be to drag that garbage can over."

"Good thinking, Officer Grieg!" said McGurk. "So why don't you do it now? Let's see just how well it would work."

Wanda didn't hesitate. Anything to do with climbing is just her bag. So she dragged the garbage can across, stood on it, and—sure enough—it brought her head level with the bare spindle.

"Okay," said McGurk. "Now you try, Officer Yoshimura."

Mari stood on the can. Her head never even reached the garage roof.

"Could you touch the top of the spike thing?" McGurk asked.

"I will try, Chief McGurk."

Mari's fingers didn't quite make it.

"Right," said McGurk. "So if the perpetrator *was* a kid, he or she would have to be taller than Officer Yoshimura."

"But there have been other weathervanes stolen, Chief McGurk," said Mari, jumping down. "Some of which maybe were higher. Too high even for someone as tall as Wanda or Willie. Even with garbage can."

"Sure!" said McGurk. "But we'll be checking on that. And if it did need a stepladder to reach some of them, that'll rule out kids. Kids under sixteen, anyway."

"How's that, McGurk?" asked Willie.

"Because they'd need transportation for the ladder. Which means a car, at least."

"Unless the *other* victims had left ladders handy," said Brains.

"We'll see," said McGurk. "You mentioned something about a panel with lights?"

"Yes," said Brains. He opened the garage door. "On the wall there."

The panel board was fixed in a rough, lopsided way. A mess of different-colored wires straggled up from behind it to a hole in the ceiling. Some small, colored bulbs were screwed into the panel in a wobbly circular pattern.

"They light up according to the wind direction," said Brains. "The top one is North, the—"

"Yeah, sure! But the crime, Officer Bellingham, the *crime*. Did the perpetrators mess with any of this?"

"How could they? The garage was locked. Anyway, it was the vane they were after, obviously."

I grinned.

"So we can rule out espionage, McGurk."

"Huh?"

"Spies," I said. "Sent by a foreign power to steal Brains's invention. I just bet they could use something like this on a missile launching site."

A dreamy look had crept into McGurk's eyes. But now he scowled.

"This is no joke, Officer Rockaway!"

"No!" growled Brains.

I sighed.

"Okay," I said, getting out my notebook. "What did it look like, anyway?"

Brains blushed.

"Well, it wasn't much to look at. I mean, I cut it out myself from a sheet of tin." His blush deepened. "Well—look—maybe it would help if you saw the plans."

He tugged a wad of paper from his back pocket. Graph paper. Several sheets of it, folded tight. Turning his back on us, he shuffled through them secretively, then handed me one.

"Blueprint of the basic weathervane," he muttered.

Blueprint of a disaster area would have been a better description. The page was covered with diagrams, figures, calculations, crossings-out, oily fingerprints, candy smears—a mess. Eventually, I made out the outline of something in the center.

"That it?" I said, tracing it with my finger.

"Of course!" snapped Brains. "What else could it be? And mind you copy it carefully!"

Well, I tried. And, believe me, it wasn't easy. Here's the result:

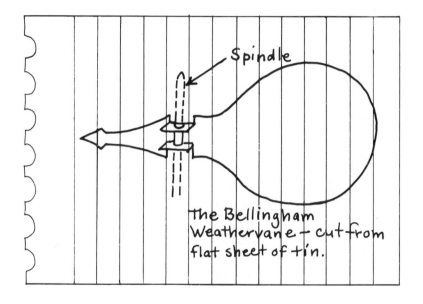

"Like that?" I said.

"Yeah—roughly," said Brains.

The others were staring at my copy.

"You call that a weathervane?" said Wanda. "*That* shape?"

"They come in all shapes," said Brains. "Fishes, birds—all shapes."

"So what's *yours* supposed to be?" said Wanda. "A fry pan?"

"Looks more like a perfume bottle to me," said Willie. "Laid on its side."

"Or a Ping-Pong paddle?" said Mari.

"Or a lollipop?" I said.

McGurk growled. "I don't care if it was supposed to represent a *magnifying glass*! Just so it's a reasonably accurate picture. Is it, Officer Bellingham?"

"Well—yeah . . ." said Brains. "I guess . . ."

"Okay, then!" said McGurk. "So now maybe we can—"

"And as a matter of fact, it *was* supposed to look like a magnifying glass," said Brains sadly. "In honor of the McGurk Organization."

"Oh, really?" murmured McGurk. "Well—uh— nice touch, Officer Bellingham. . . . So now let's see if we can't get it back to you, huh? And soon. . . . Where else on this street were the other two swiped from?"

"I'll show you," said Brains.

3 The Jinxed Submarine

The first we came to was a ranch house. This time, the bare spindle was on the roof of the house. The four letters stood out large and bold: N, S, E, and W.

"It was shaped like a pig," said Brains.

McGurk went into his height-gauging routine.

"*Fairly* easy to get at," he murmured. "What do you think, Officer Grieg?"

"Sure!" Wanda replied. "No problem. Maybe a garbage can wouldn't be tall enough, this time. But an ordinary stepladder would get you onto the porch roof—and the rest would be easy."

"Hm!" McGurk gave her a beady look. "Do *you* have a stepladder in your garage?"

"Yes, but—" Wanda stopped. "Hey, now look! I know just what you're thinking! But do you realize how many older kids in this town have drivers' licenses? Besides Ed?"

"All right, all right!" said McGurk. "All I was saying is that it's now in the older-kid category. Which means some kind of prank. It obviously wasn't a professional cat burglar job."

"How d'you know that, McGurk?" said Willie.

"Well, take a look across the street," said McGurk. "I don't remember ever noticing the pig that was swiped—"

"How unobservant!" said Wanda. "*I* do."

"Be quiet!" snapped McGurk, flushing. "I was going to say I don't remember it in all its dumb details. But what I *am* quite sure of is that it was never in the same league as that rooster up there."

We looked across at the roof of a three-story house. The golden weathercock gleamed bright against the dull clouds, veering slightly from west to north even as we stared.

"That's probably ten times more valuable than the pig," said McGurk. "But it stays and the pig gets swiped."

"Listen, fellas, please don't stare so much!" said Brains. "That's Mr. Van Cleef's house. He gets kind of grouchy when kids hang around like this. . . .

Besides, *he* hasn't been robbed. It's the folks over here, the Wentworths—"

"You're right, Officer Bellingham," said McGurk, turning back to the ranch house. "Let's get a few more details about the missing pig."

He rang the doorbell three times, but no one answered.

"All right," he said. "We'll try them later. Which was the other place?"

"Farther along. Mr. and Mrs. Getzoff's house. Mrs. Getzoff's a friend of Mom's," Brains added, leading the way.

This was another place where the weathervane had been mounted on the garage roof. Again the bare spike looked forlorn.

"Wasn't this in the shape of a ship of some kind?" said McGurk.

"Well, a submarine, to be exact," said Brains. "I think it was supposed to be the *Nautilus,* the first nuclear-powered—"

"Whatever!" McGurk grunted. "There's somebody home here, anyway."

A tall young man was standing on the doorstep, talking to someone just inside. He was writing in a notebook.

"Hey!" I said. "It's Mark Westover, from the *Gazette!*"

He'd even interviewed *us* once, when we'd cracked the case of the Felon's Fiddle.

"Maybe he can tell us about some of the other weathervanes," said McGurk, moving forward.

"Wait until he's finished talking with Mr. Getzoff, then!" said Brains.

"Oh—uh—sure . . ." muttered McGurk.

"So how much would you say it was worth?" the reporter was asking.

"Oh, not a lot!" said Mr. Getzoff. He's a small guy with big, sad brown eyes but a smiling mouth. He didn't look exactly heartbroken over his loss. "It cost us a hundred and fifty dollars—but I think we were robbed even *then*! Anyway, it was jinxed."

"Jinxed?" said Mark Westover.

"Yeah, well," said Mr. Getzoff, "the guy who sold it to us got killed the same day. In a car crash. Skidded off the highway and dove thirty feet down the embankment into a river."

"Really?" Mark Westover was scribbling away again.

"Yeah. And not only that—the ghouls must have gotten wind of his death."

A kind of shudder went through us at the word "ghouls."

"Ghouls?" said Mark Westover.

"Yeah! You know. The usual creeps. The poor guy's body must only just have reached the morgue when thieves broke into his house and ransacked it. It was in the papers the next day."

"Interesting," Mark Westover murmured. "And so you think the weathervane itself was jinxed."

Mr. Getzoff shrugged.

"Oh, well . . . you know. It makes you wonder. I mean . . . well . . ."

"Did *you* have anything bad happen to you?"

"No! Nothing like that, thank goodness! But—" Mr. Getzoff grinned uneasily. "Well, I've had a pretty lousy run of luck in the state lottery, ever since."

Mark Westover smiled.

"Maybe if I mention the jinx, whoever took it might return it fast!"

"Just as you please," said Mr. Getzoff. "Personally, they can keep it, for all I care."

McGurk growled. He hates for people to give up on getting back anything stolen from them. "It only encourages the thieves!" he once said.

Mr. Getzoff must have heard the growl. He looked out.

"What do you kids want?" he said. Then he recognized Brains. "Do *you* know anything about this, Gerald?"

Before Brains could answer, Mark Westover had recognized the rest of us.

"Hi, McGurk!" he said. "It's okay, Mr. Getzoff. I can vouch for these guys. They're probably investigating the crime themselves."

"We sure are, Mr. Westover!" said McGurk, stepping forward. "And maybe you could fill us in on a few—"

Brains interrupted.

"I'm a victim myself!"

"Really?" said Mark Westover. "Tell me about it. There are some very interesting aspects to this case. We're getting calls from all over town from people who've had their weathervanes stolen. And there's no firm pattern."

Brains told the reporter about his own loss, showing him a page or two of his "blueprints."

Mark Westover's eyebrows went up as he glanced at them.

"Like I said," he murmured, "no real pattern. All kinds of weathervanes have disappeared. Some expensive, some—uh—just junk."

"Any pattern in location, though?" said McGurk.

"Not really," said the reporter. "Maybe a few more in this area than in other parts. It's early yet to—"

"I meant like in height," said McGurk. "Like being easy to reach."

"Ah, you mean *accessibility*," said Mark Westover. "Now you mention it, all those I've been inquiring into so far *have* been fairly low. Garage roofs, sheds, ranch houses, that kind of thing."

"That's what I was figuring," said McGurk, looking pleased. Then that look faded as the reporter turned to Brains and said, "Your name's Bellingham, right? With two *l*'s?"

"Hey, Mr. Westover!" said McGurk. "You're not going to mention *him* being a victim, are you?"

"Two *l*'s," said Brains. "First name, Ger—"

"Hold it!" snapped McGurk, glowering at Brains. Then he turned back to the reporter, a strained, pleading look in his eyes. "You're not *really* going to—?"

"Sure!" said Mark Westover. "Why not? It'll make a good human-interest angle. 'Member of local detective organization among the victims . . .' "

"But, Mr. Westover—"

The reporter's pen became still. His eyes were cold as they looked down at McGurk.

"You're not asking me to suppress a news item, are you, McGurk?"

Even our leader couldn't stand up to the quiet menace in that tone and those eyes.

"Uh—well—no—of course not," he muttered.

But he let poor Brains have it a few minutes later, just before we broke for lunch.

"Why did you have to tell him about *your* weathervane, Officer Bellingham?"

"Well—it *was* stolen, wasn't it?"

"Sure! But now we just *have* to solve the case. And in record time. Before that article appears. Otherwise, everyone in town will be laughing at us, you dummy!"

Patrolman Cassidy's
4 Warning

Straight after lunch, we went on a tour of the immediate neighborhood, checking on houses where we'd heard of weathervanes being taken, or where we saw the telltale bare spindles. And, boy, had those thieves (or pranksters) been busy!

Counting those we already knew about, we'd collected a list of twelve by three o'clock.

"Right, men!" McGurk said. "That's enough for openers." He glanced at my notebook. It was crowded with names, addresses, descriptions. "And let's concentrate on the most important details."

His idea of doing this was for us to go back to headquarters and for me to type out a list, with a copy for each officer.

"Then we'll be able to see the pattern more clearly," he said.

Well, it didn't take long, and here it is:

Weathervanes Taken Locally
Friday Night, Oct. 31

SHAPE	VALUE	POSITION
Magnifying Glass	N.R.V.	Garage roof
Pig	$150?	Ranch house roof
Submarine	$150	Garage roof
Running Fox	?	Garage roof
Gabriel Blowing Horn	$3000	Ranch house roof
Mermaid	$1000	Pool house roof
Rooster	$100	Garden shed roof
Rooster	?	Gazebo roof
Flying Fish	$850	Ranch house roof
Stagecoach & Horses	$500	Ranch house roof
Yacht	?	Garage roof
Witch Riding Broomstick	$350	Ranch house roof

N.R.V. stands for No Retail Value. I had to put that because Brains was all for claiming *his* weathervane to be worth $20,000, as part of a very valuable invention—and the resulting argument looked like it could go on all afternoon. The $3,000 Gabriel weathervane was the one on East Elm that we'd already heard about. It was a genuine seventeenth-century antique—but I'm not sure about the value of many of the others. In some cases the owners weren't in, so the figures were based on what the neighbors *thought* the value might be. And where no one seemed to have any idea about the value, I just put a question mark.

McGurk had his doubts about most of them.

"Victims often exaggerate the prices," he said. "On account of the insurance claims. I bet some of those wouldn't have rated fifty cents in a garage sale," he added, giving Brains a dirty look.

"Anyway," he continued, "what it boils down to is this. There was no picking and choosing by the *perps*. Some of the weathervanes were very valuable, yes, but many weren't. So, like I've said all along, this has all the signs of a prank."

"Yes," said Wanda. "*I* think it's a prank, too."

We all stared at her. This was unexpected. McGurk looked relieved.

"Good! I'm glad you're not letting family ties come between you and an investigation, Officer Grieg. Because, after all, with stunts like this, you just have to think Ed Grieg."

"Sure!" said Wanda. "And I've been thinking about *that*, also. And I've come to the conclusion that Ed had no part in it."

McGurk's look of relief was replaced by one of deep suspicion.

"Oh? Why? Does he have an alibi for last night?"

"I'm not thinking about alibis, McGurk. I'm thinking about the M.O. The method of operation. It just isn't Ed's style."

"Oh, no?"

"No. If Ed had done it, he'd have done it in spades. *He'd* have gone for the golden rooster on Mr. Van Cleef's house."

McGurk wasn't buying *that*!

"Come on, Officer Grieg! The Van Cleef weathervane is three stories high. It would need a builder's ladder to get up there, and that would need a truck, not just a car."

But Wanda was shaking her head.

"That's all *you* know, McGurk! But I can tell you this. All that would be necessary would be an ordinary stepladder."

"Oh, yeah?"

"Yeah! Who's the climbing expert around here, anyway?"

McGurk had no answer to that.

"But—"

"Why don't we go there now?" said Wanda. "And I'll show you."

So, for the second time that day, we all stood outside the Van Cleef house, gazing up at the bright golden rooster. This time it looked even higher and more inaccessible.

"*That*," said Wanda, "would have been a challenge to Ed. And Ed has never been able to resist a challenge."

"Yes, but *how*, Wanda?" said Mari. "How could he have climbed up *there*?"

"Yeah," said McGurk. "How? And with only a stepladder, remember?"

Wanda took a few paces forward, onto the Van Cleef driveway.

"See that porch?" she said. "At the side? The

stepladder would have gotten him onto the roof of that with no trouble at all."

"Then what?" said Willie.

"Just step over here, more to the side," said Wanda.

"Now—see that drainpipe running past the window above the porch? . . . Well, notice that that window juts out, with its own little roof. Step number two."

We gaped. I for one was seeing this in a whole different light. Like pale moonlight. With the tall shadowy figure of Ed Grieg already swarming up past the second story.

"Now," said Wanda, "you'll notice a ledge running around the house just above that window. Three or four sideways steps along that ledge bring you level with that turret thing, right? Right! So all he has to do then is grab hold of the windowsill and hoist himself up."

"Oh, but he will fall!" gasped Mari.

"Not my brother!" said Wanda. "Not Grieg the Greatest! The champion all-around athlete of his class!"

"Go on!" said McGurk. "I'm beginning to see what you mean. So next he just—?"

"Hauls himself onto the roof, yes," said Wanda. "And now it's a cinch. He reaches out and—"

"*What are you doing there?*"

The harsh, thin voice cut into our imaginary pictures like we'd been up there ourselves, in the moonlight, and suddenly we'd been caught in the act.

Brains groaned. It was Mr. Van Cleef. He looked *furious.*

"Get off my property!" he snarled, without waiting for an answer. "Now! Before I call the police!"

We nearly fell over each other in our haste to do as he said.

"Wow!" gasped Willie. "Was *he* all steamed up!"

"I guess it did look kind of suspicious," said Wanda.

"He's probably nervous about *his* weathervane," I said.

"Anyway," said McGurk, always the first to recover, "talking of police, look who's here!"

We'd just turned into Hickory Avenue—one of the streets we hadn't checked earlier, since we don't usually count it as part of the immediate neighborhood. McGurk was pointing to a patrol car parked farther along, outside a ranch house. One with a bare spindle and four lonely letters on its roof.

"Oh, good!" said Mari. "It is Mr. Cassidy!"

Even in her short time with us, she'd come to know and trust the cop with the gray mustache, who was talking to a woman at the front door. Patrolman Cassidy was in fact a special friend of the McGurk Organization's. We had no hesitation in walking across and waiting for him at the end of the driveway.

"Okay," he was saying, reading over his notes. "That's another fox design, huh?"

"Hounds chasing a fox, yes," said the lady.

"And it went missing last night?"

"Correct."

"Would you care to put a price on it, ma'am?"

"Yes, I would!" said the woman. "This morning, when I was talking to the newspaper person, I thought it was worth about two hundred dollars.

Now I understand it's worth more than twice that. It's an absolute disgrace!"

"I understand, ma'am. It *is* annoying. But we're doing everything we can."

As he approached the gate, Mr. Cassidy gave a big sigh. He looked like he'd just been given a hard time. His face didn't relax much when he saw us. He seemed to have only just enough good humor left to greet McGurk with his usual joke.

"Hi, McKirk! I haven't time to talk now. Sorry!"

McGurk didn't bother to correct him.

"But *we're* investigating this weathervane thing, too, Mr. Cassidy. We—"

"Oh, yeah?" Mr. Cassidy had stopped. "Well, just take a tip from me. Keep out of this one, M'Turk!

Folks are getting mad. Real mad. It's no use telling them the vanes'll soon start showing up again—that it's probably just some student prank."

The cop's shrewd eyes fell on Wanda. Wanda blushed. McGurk nodded.

"Yes. That's what I've been thinking, too. But—"

"But stay out of it!" growled Mr. Cassidy. "Hear? Prank or no prank, it's creating a lot of bad feeling. County HQ are already leaning on us, what with Election Day coming up and all. And Lieutenant Kaspar is getting fit to be tied." The cop gave another weary sigh. "So keep out of it, McGurk, because—believe me—the lieutenant is going to throw the book at the perpetrators this time, kid stuff or not!"

"But we're only—"

"Only investigating, yeah! *I* know that and *you* know that. But all the angry, ripped-off taxpayer sees is a bunch of kids!"

"Yes, sir," said Mari. "We already have been treated with suspicion."

"There you are, then," said Patrolman Cassidy. "See what I mean, McGurk?"

McGurk swallowed hard.

"We'll keep a low profile, Mr. Cassidy," he said.

"So make sure it *is* low, huh?" said Mr. Cassidy, getting back into the car.

5 Number-One Suspect?

"You're not the only one who's decided to keep a low profile, McGurk," I said, a few minutes later, when we walked up the Grieg driveway.

Ed Grieg *was* keeping a low profile. Literally.

All we could see of him were the soles of his size-12 sneakers, sticking out from under his old VW Beetle in the garage.

"Ed," said Wanda, "can you come out from under for a second?"

"No," came the grunted reply.

"Ed, it's important!"

"Beat it!" Ed growled.

McGurk pushed forward.

"It's in your best interests, Ed. This is Jack McGurk—"

"I don't have time to talk to kids!"

"But it's official business, Ed," McGurk persisted. "We're investigating this weathervane thing."

"I'm busy! Beat it!"

McGurk sighed, then frowned. In a sterner, slower voice, he said, "We've just been talking to Patrolman Cassidy. He says the police are going to get tough. Prank or no prank, Lieutenant Kaspar is going to treat it as a felony and—"

"*What?!*"

Ed had been lying on one of those flat boards on wheels. At the word "felony," he shot out from under on it and sent us scattering.

"*What* did you say?" he growled, leaping to his feet in one swift movement.

There was no doubt about *his* being in peak athletic condition.

The oily streaks on his face made him look ferocious. That and the wrench in his hand and his bristly gunfighter mustache. He looks more like a twenty-eight-year-old than a high-school kid of eighteen, and I couldn't help thinking that if he *was* nailed for this caper, no judge would feel like taking his youth into account when dishing out the sentence.

McGurk repeated what Mr. Cassidy had told us. Ed's oil-streaked T-shirt heaved in time with his breathing.

"What's this got to do with *me*?" he said.

"Well—"

"Look!" Ed glanced at his watch, then at his oil-smudged arms. "I have to take a shower. Wait here and I'll be right back."

When Ed had gone indoors, McGurk started prowling around the garage. It was pretty tidy. There were no old tea chests full of junk, or piles of stuff in corners. No place where a bunch of weathervanes could be hidden, in fact. But there *was* a folded stepladder, hanging from a wall bracket. McGurk felt the legs at the bottom.

"What's that for, McGurk?" said Willie.

"To see if there's any caked mud. Or dampness. Any sign it might have been used outdoors recently. Sniff it, Officer Sandowsky. Any crushed grass smell?"

"You never give up, do you, McGurk?" Wanda said, as Willie applied his ultrasensitive nose to the stepladder, then shook his head.

McGurk turned to Wanda.

"The way things are shaping up, Ed Grieg looks like he'll be in big trouble," he said.

"And *you* want to be the one to land him in it up to his neck, huh?" said Wanda.

A peculiar look crossed McGurk's face: half-angry, half terribly worried. And it was then that I realized how close the Organization was to being torn apart.

"We want to be the ones to get him out of the mess, Officer Grieg!" McGurk said. "If he really *hasn't* had anything to do with it."

Wanda glared at McGurk.

"And if he *has*, I suppose you're still going to turn him in. Right?"

"If he *has*—well . . ." McGurk's shoulders slumped. "Well, I *was* going to make an exception and walk away from the case. Leave it to the cops. On account that the suspect is the brother of an Organization officer."

"Oh, yeah?" said Wanda, but less fiercely.

"Yes," McGurk said, sort of sadly. "But now that Mark Westover is going to name one of us in his article"—here, McGurk shot Brains a withering glance—"as a *victim*—well—we don't have a choice. We just have to go on and try to bust the case ourselves."

This time it was Wanda who threw a scowl at Brains. Then she sighed.

"Ed was always your number-one suspect though, wasn't he, McGurk?"

"Yeah. *Was*. And you can bet he already *is* the cops' number-one suspect, Officer Grieg! Did you notice the way Mr. Cassidy looked at you when he was talking about pranks? We have to stay on this case if only to prove Ed's innocence."

Mari looked up.

"Are you saying that Ed is no longer *your* number-one suspect, Chief McGurk?"

"Well"—McGurk was frowning thoughtfully—"certain things are already making me doubt it. Like Officer Grieg's point about it not being Ed's style. And—well—something else."

"Like what?" I asked, noticing the gleam in his eyes.

He shook his head.

"Right now it's only in the hunch stage. Right now the main thing is to talk to Ed. . . . He's taking a long time over that shower, isn't he?"

"Yes," said Wanda, alert and bright again. "I'll try to get him to hurry it along."

I breathed a sigh of relief. It looked like the storm was passing us by. The McGurk Organization was working as a team once more.

But then, a couple of minutes later, that internal weathervane of mine veered right back in the storm direction.

Wanda looked pale as she came hurrying back.

"I'm sorry, McGurk! He—he's gone!"

"Gone?"

"He's taken his shower and gone out the back way. He told Mom he wouldn't be back until late!"

McGurk scowled.

"Huh! That looks bad!"

"What do you mean?" said Wanda, bristling again.

"I mean it looks like genuine guilt, Officer Grieg—that's what!"

6 Ed Grants an Audience

Fortunately, it was getting dark and we had to go home, so McGurk and Wanda had the whole of Saturday night to cool off.

And when we met again the next morning, Brains delivered another bombshell—one that blew everything else out of our minds.

He was only a couple of minutes late this time.

"Hey!" he gasped, as he burst into the basement. "Someone came in the night and replaced the weathervane. Only—"

"You mean *your* weathervane?" said McGurk. "On your garage roof?"

"Well, no. Not exactly. I—"

"So what are you talking about, Officer Bellingham?"

"Well—they put a weathervane back on the spindle, all right, but it isn't *mine*. It is one of the roosters!"

"So!" said McGurk. "It really *is* a prank. Just the kind of prank—" He glanced at Wanda. She was glaring at him, fists clenched. He must have decided it would be wiser to drop that line. "So why didn't you bring it along here, Officer Bellingham? This rooster. It could be valuable evidence."

"It sure could!" said Brains. "And I was going to. But Mom had already reported it to the police, and they said not to touch it until the fingerprint guys had checked it."

"Wow!" said Willie. "They really do mean business!"

The rest of us nodded. Wanda looked worried. She no longer looked so feisty at *this* piece of news.

"Any others?" snapped McGurk.

"Yes," said Brains. "Next door. The Wentworths have gotten the mermaid on theirs. And the Getzoffs now have a yacht instead of a submarine."

"Have *all* the weathervanes been restored?" McGurk asked. "Mixed up or not?"

Brains shook his head.

"No. On my way here, I noticed the one on East

Elm, the three-thousand-dollar one, was still missing. And Mrs. Getzoff told Mom there were still some bare spindles over in the Willow Park area."

McGurk turned to Wanda. Very gently, he said, "Listen, Wanda—this could still look bad for Ed. Where is he now?"

Two tears suddenly welled up in her eyes.

"In—in bed," she murmured. "He's resting."

"Resting, huh?"

That brought Wanda to more like her usual self.

"He always *does* rest, Sunday mornings! Athletes require it!"

McGurk lifted his hands.

"Sure, sure! Simmer down! And just listen to some common sense, Officer Grieg! This time we *have* to talk to him. Because if he doesn't cooperate, it looks like he'll get more rest than he needs."

"Oh?" said Wanda, no longer defiant.

"Yeah!" said McGurk. "On his bunk. In a cell. In the county jail. Now take us to him, please!"

Wanda didn't argue anymore. Five minutes later, we were invited into Ed's room—like he was some kind of king who'd invited a bunch of serfs in for an audience.

"I suppose you've come to ask about this dumb weathervane stunt?" he said, as we stood gazing down at him from the foot of the bed.

He looked even taller that way, stretched out full-length under the covers, with his head and shoulders propped against the pillows. He'd been reading the sports section of the Sunday paper, and it was spread open in front of him. The other sections lay on the floor, untouched.

"Yes," said McGurk. "We have. And it's very important."

"Important!" Ed let out a bellow of laughter. "That's what *she* said!" he went on, giving a mere nod at the sister who'd been pitching for him so

valiantly. "You kids! You really amuse me sometimes! Wow! Some dumb stunt and you say
important!"

McGurk let him have his chuckle out. Then:

"It *is* important, Ed. The police think so. They—"

"Listen!" growled Ed, suddenly sitting up and
stabbing a finger at McGurk. "Grow up! The weathervanes haven't been stolen. They'll all be returned.
Some have been. Already. Maybe they've been
mixed up some, but"—he shrugged and grinned—
"heck! So what? It makes it all the more fun."

"You mean you did it?" gasped Wanda.

"Me? Naw! I admit it's the sort of thing I *used* to
do. When I was a kid. Only better—naturally." Ed's
grin faded. His eyes narrowed. "*Now* what? What're
you staring at me like that for?"

McGurk blinked.

"So you know about that, huh?"

"About what?"

"About some of the weathervanes turning up
again. In the wrong places."

"Sure! I just said so, didn't I?"

McGurk's eyes gleamed.

"But you haven't gotten up yet. You haven't even
left this room, I bet. So *how* do you know?"

Ed laughed again.

"Oh, boy! McGurk! I'm surprised at you! See

this?" He reached out to the floor, behind the pile of newspaper sections, and came back up with a red telephone.

"Ah!" said Mari, nodding.

"Yeah—ah!" Ed crowed. "This little kid here has more brights than you, McGurk. She knows that this thing is called a telephone. You can use it to talk to people without leaving your bed. And I have friends. Some of them call me. I call them. That's how telephones work. You should try it sometime, McGurk. Only"—Ed's eyes glinted—"don't call *me*. I'll call *you*. Now beat it, before—"

Just then the phone rang, making us all jump, Ed included. But he hung on to the instrument and plunged with it under the covers. Again all in one movement.

We stared at the hump in the bed covers.

"Hi!" came his muffled voice.

McGurk stepped forward, unashamed, and bent his head. I guess he felt that after the insults the suspect had just heaped on him he had every right to pick up whatever scrap of information he could.

But he needn't have bothered. Ed's voice was clear enough even through the sheets and blankets.

"Oh, it's *you*, Mealy! Look, I can't talk right now. I'll get back to you later."

There was the clunk of the receiver being replaced, and Ed emerged once more, scowling at the phone and muttering, "Jerk!" Then he saw us.

"You still here?"

"Yes," said McGurk. "But—"

"Go!" Ed growled. "Now! Directly! Pronto! Immediately!"

He began to rear up, like King Neptune from the waves.

We went.

Wanda looked dismayed and embarrassed. I guess we all did. All except McGurk.

His face was slightly flushed, yes. But his green eyes were glowing with satisfaction as we left that room.

7 Hunches

I could guess the cause of that look on McGurk's face. Key word: "Mealy."

Mealy Oates is one of Ed's hangers-on. He's the same age as Ed but three-fourths his size. He isn't an athlete himself, but he's starry-eyed about Ed's feats. He even tries to copy Ed in other ways. Like driving around in a battered old VW and trying to grow a mustache. The mustache is a laugh—a few droopy hairs—but Mealy himself is a pain.

Could it be that Mealy had pulled the weather-vane caper and had blown it, and now Ed was trying to bail him out, feeling kind of responsible? Was *this* McGurk's latest hunch?

"Another lead, McGurk?" I said, as we left the Grieg house.

"Could be," he grunted. "But we need to collect more hard evidence. And first we have to see which weathervanes have turned up again."

"Yes," said Mari. "And *where* they turned up."

"And which are still missing," Brains added, wistfully.

Well, it wasn't easy. The police were already active, removing any weathervanes that had been replaced during the night, and taking them back for fingerprint checks. As a result we could never be sure when we saw a bare spindle whether the owners had had a substitute and the cops had removed it, or they'd not yet received a replacement of *any* kind.

So we had to ask the victims themselves or their neighbors—and people were getting tired of answering questions. Mark Westover had already been covering this new development. Also we noticed a TV van doing the rounds.

Anyway, it took us the rest of the morning and most of the afternoon to bring our information up-to-date. Here's a copy of the summary I made:

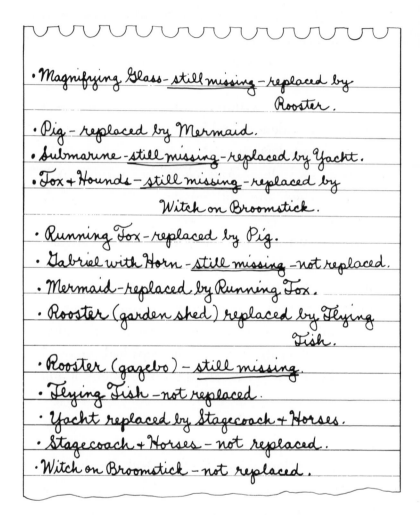

- Magnifying Glass- still missing - replaced by Rooster.
- Pig - replaced by Mermaid.
- Submarine - still missing - replaced by Yacht.
- Fox + Hounds - still missing - replaced by Witch on Broomstick.
- Running Fox - replaced by Pig.
- Gabriel with Horn - still missing - not replaced.
- Mermaid - replaced by Running Fox.
- Rooster (garden shed) replaced by Flying Fish.
- Rooster (gazebo) - still missing.
- Flying Fish - not replaced.
- Yacht replaced by Stagecoach + Horses.
- Stagecoach + Horses - not replaced.
- Witch on Broomstick - not replaced.

There are thirteen weathervanes on this list instead of the original twelve because we added the one we'd found out about later—the Fox and Hounds.

"Hm," murmured McGurk, when he studied the list. "Interesting! *Very* interesting!"

"*What's* interesting, McGurk?" said Wanda. "Do you see a pattern or something?"

"Negative," said McGurk. "There is no pattern. That's what's so interesting. Some of the five still missing are pretty junky, while others are worth hundreds of dollars—thousands, in the case of the Gabriel thing."

"Yes," said Mari. "But you will notice that the second most valuable, the Mermaid, *has* been brought back, Chief McGurk."

"Yeah," murmured McGurk. "Which *seems* to rule out a professional job."

"I thought you'd ruled that out already," said Wanda.

"I said 'seems,' Officer Grieg. And I don't rule out *anything*, ever, until I have *all* the evidence."

"Anyway," I said, "maybe some more will turn up tonight."

"Maybe," said McGurk. "We'll soon see, anyway."

Well, he was right to be doubtful. Because what we did soon see was the surprise item toward the end of the six-o'clock TV news.

"And now," said the anchorwoman, "here's something that happened in one corner of our area

that's getting a lot of residents in a—uh—spin. It *could* be called The Case of the Wandering Weathervanes."

I sat bolt upright as the camera cut to a street in our town and zoomed in on the roof of a ranch house, focusing on the bare spindle.

I craned forward, and as soon as the camera came down to the doorway, I recognized the lady standing there. It was the one on Hickory. And she was looking even madder.

"Yes!" she said. "That was a beautiful rare antique weathervane. Hounds chasing a fox. Worth over a thousand dollars!"

(Boy! I thought. The price is going up by the hour!)

"But wasn't it replaced?" asked the TV guy.

"Oh, sure! By a hunk of junk! A witch on a broom-stick—a real cheap—"

"Yes, ma'am," said the interviewer, "but where is it now?"

"The police took it," said the lady. "To check for fingerprints. And I hope when they find who did it they'll not go soft and give him a slap on the wrist!"

The reporter turned to the camera.

"That's the way most of the victims are taking it," he said. "One resident, however, is much more philosophical. . . ."

The camera cut to another bare spindle—this time on top of a garage. And when it tracked down, who should be there but Mr. Getzoff!

He was already talking.

"Well, the more I think of it, the more I'm sure the thing was jinxed."

"Yours was shaped like a submarine, I believe?"

"Yeah. And it was jinxed."

"What makes you say that, sir?"

"The attitude of the guy who sold it to us, mainly. I can remember it clearly—one summer afternoon in a little town near Mystic Seaport. He was sweat-ing and trembling. My wife thought he was sick, right, Meg?"

Cut to Mrs. Getzoff, nodding.

"She asked if he was all right or should we leave,"

continued Mr. Getzoff. "But the guy wouldn't hear of it. What he did, though, was put the CLOSED notice on the door and lock it. Even though another customer was already coming up the steps. Even when the guy started knocking, the store owner wouldn't open up. 'Just take your time,' he said to us. But he was still shaking, and when we said we'd take the submarine he looked relieved, like he was glad to be rid of it."

"And after you bought it," said the interviewer, "you heard he'd been killed?"

"Yes," said Mr. Getzoff. "That same afternoon. Within an hour or so. We were his very last customers."

"And you haven't had much luck since then?"

"Well—" Mr. Getzoff began.

"Terrible!" said Mrs. Getzoff.

The interviewer turned to face the camera.

"So if anyone out there has that weathervane, they'd best beware! Jinx or no jinx, it will certainly bring them bad luck if the local police catch them with it!"

This time the camera cut to the outside of the town's police station and a tall man with a smooth, bright pink face and piercing blue eyes: Lieutenant Kaspar himself.

And was he mad!

We of the McGurk Organization know only too well that the angrier he gets, the pinker his face becomes and the deeper blue are his eyes. My dad reached forward to adjust the color, but he was wasting his time. It wasn't the set's fault.

"I have only one comment to make," Lieutenant Kaspar said, scowling straight at the camera. "We are treating this matter as a criminal offense. And when we apprehend the perpetrator or perpetrators, he, she, or they will be prosecuted to the full extent of the law!"

It was a chilling statement. The anchorwoman underlined it.

"So there we are. Whichever way the wind happens to be blowing right now in that corner of our state, those perpetrators can be sure of a blast of cold Arctic air coming their way before long. And talking of winds, let's go to our weatherman. . . . Pete?"

She turned, smiling, to a smiling weatherman.

But *I* wasn't smiling. And I knew someone else who wouldn't be, if she'd been watching.

Sure enough, about ten minutes later, Wanda called, sounding terribly worried.

"Did you see it, Joey?"

"Yes," I said. "And—"

"Didn't Lieutenant Kaspar look mad?!"

"He sure did! I guess he's like McGurk. He feels he just *can't* treat it as a joke now."

"No. . . ."

I heard Wanda gulp.

"Er—they haven't pulled Ed in for questioning, have they?" I asked.

"No. As a matter of fact, he went to the police station himself, voluntarily, this afternoon. He said he'd heard about the fingerprints and offered them a sample of his own."

"So—*did* they find any that matched?"

"They didn't say. But I'm sure they won't. Ed *is* innocent, you know!"

"I wonder what McGurk will say, when he hears?"

"He already has!" said Wanda. "I called him a

few minutes ago." She made a sniffling sound. "He said it didn't mean a thing. Even if the prints didn't match. He said that Ed could have been wearing gloves when he took the weathervanes back. And— and the cops will think the same."

I could tell she was close to crying.

"Hey, Wanda!" I said. "*I* think Ed is innocent. And I'm sure McGurk does, too. We both had the same hunch today—I think."

"Oh? What hunch?"

"I only said I *think* we did. . . . Just don't worry. I'll see you in school tomorrow."

Ed and the
8 Lie-Detector

There were no weathervanes returned *that* night. I mean, after Lieutenant Kaspar's TV announcement, it would have taken a very dumb perpetrator to go around in the dark toting a bunch of weathervanes!

Another result was that the next morning the school principal broadcast over the public address system asking for anyone who might have had anything to do with the caper to come tell him about it. "Because, believe me," he ended, "it will be much better than if the police have to come to *you!*"

No one went to the office, and McGurk said he wasn't surprised.

"This was strictly a *high-school* student operation," he said. "Either that or a professional adult job."

"So you really haven't ruled that out?" I said.

"No. I—"

And that was when Miss Johnson told us to stop talking in class.

McGurk didn't bring it up again later when we were free to talk. Instead, he had us working hard during breaks and all through the lunch period, questioning kids from other parts of town about the weathervanes that had gone missing in their areas. As a result, I compiled a list of eleven weathervanes—including such shapes as a leaping stag, a flying goose, turkeys (2), a soaring eagle, and a running hare. I won't present a copy of that list here— it wouldn't be relevant. What *was* relevant was the note I made at the end:

WEATHERVANES FROM ELSEWHERE
IN TOWN (continued)

N.B. Not a single one has
yet been returned – even on
Saturday night.

McGurk himself underlined those last four words, after school, back in his basement.

"Now that *is* interesting!" he murmured. "At least it tells us *something* about the perpetrator."

We looked at each other. McGurk had lost us this time.

"Go on, McGurk!" said Wanda.

"It tells us," said McGurk, sitting back, slitty-eyed, "that he must live in our neighborhood."

Brains gasped.

"You mean—"

"I mean that when he did take a risk and start putting some back, he wasn't prepared to go far. He didn't want to cover too much territory and risk being stopped by a patrolman."

"Yeah!" said Willie. "Maybe he didn't even bother using his car. Maybe he took the weathervanes out one at a time, under his coat."

"Good thinking, Officer Sandowsky!"

"So how about the stepladder?" said Brains.

"Maybe," said Willie, "he was tall enough and—uh—fit enough not to need—"

He broke off, nervously fingering his nose. Wanda had turned toward him angrily.

"Cool it, Officer Grieg!" said McGurk. "A good detective has to cover every possibility. . . . Nice work, Officer Sandowsky. . . ." He turned to

Wanda again. "Anyway, I think it's time we gave your brother a lie-detector test."

Wanda sat up, startled.

"*What* lie-detector?" She glanced at the one Brains had made, but which had broken down and was lying in a corner, waiting for parts.

A slow smile spread across McGurk's face. He was looking at Mari.

"Can't you guess?" he murmured.

"Wow, yes!" gasped Willie.

"Of *course!*" said Brains.

Mari said nothing. She just sat very still, staring back at McGurk, waiting.

What we'd all been forgetting was Mari's wonderful talent for voices. I mean, not only can she throw her own voice and make her dolls talk as well as any professional ventriloquist, but she is also good at imitating other people's voices. In fact, she has an ear for voices that can detect accents, reservations, hesitations, even when the speaker is trying to cover them up.

"My brothers," she once told us, "call me the human lie-detector."

"Okay, Officer Yoshimura?" McGurk said.

"I will try, Chief McGurk," she said. "I cannot guarantee one hundred percent accuracy. But I will try. Especially," she added, glancing doubtfully at

Wanda, "if it will help to prove Ed is innocent."

"Yes, well," said Wanda, "fine! But—" she turned to McGurk—"the problem is, how do we get him to cooperate? He'll never agree to another interview."

McGurk grunted. "Yeah, that *is* a problem. Maybe—"

He broke off. The door had been flung open— and who should walk in but Ed!

"Hey, listen!" he said. "I need your help!"

"Sure!" said McGurk. "Sure! Come right in and sit down!"

Ed was "right in" already. McGurk had gotten up to close the door. And Ed did sit down.

In McGurk's chair.

It hadn't even stopped rocking.

McGurk wasn't fazed, though. He obviously preferred to stand. He was now able to make like a D.A. grilling a suspect, doing a little walking around, then suddenly turning and firing off a question.

"Okay," he began. "*How* can we help you?"

Ed wasn't intimidated. He wasn't even looking at McGurk. He was scowling at the toes of his sneakers.

"Information," he said. "You guys have an in with the police, right?"

"Well—"

"Like Patrolman Cassidy. He gave you those, didn't he?"

Ed was looking at the handcuffs hanging on the wall. Then he gave a little shudder and went back to studying his sneakers.

"Sure," said McGurk. "Mr. Cassidy is an old friend of ours, but—"

"Well, I want you to pick his brains. Talk to him. Sort of casual, like you're interested in this weathervane thing—"

"Oh, we *are!*" said McGurk. "Believe it!"

"And see what he says," Ed continued. "If he can tell you how they're doing. Any leads. Okay?"

"Sure, Ed. But why?"

Ed gave McGurk a quick scowl.

"*You* know why, McGurk! *They* suspect me just like you do."

Ed went back to the gloomy inspection of his sneakers. McGurk glanced at Mari. Mari nodded. She hunched forward, stared at Ed's face, then closed her eyes.

"Are you telling us you *didn't* take those weathervanes, Ed?" McGurk asked quietly.

"No!" snapped Ed.

A look of unbelievable cunning squirmed across McGurk's face.

"You mean, no, you are not telling us that? Or, no, you didn't take the weathervanes?"

Mari nodded approvingly.

Ed glared.

"What's with you, McGurk? I mean, no—I— did—*not*—take those weathervanes!"

"Okay, okay!" said McGurk. "Take it easy, Ed! All we're doing is just checking. If we're going to help, we need to know."

"Anyway," Ed muttered, "that's the truth."

Mari was nodding slightly.

"Sure," said McGurk. "But that's only the half of it. Maybe *you* didn't take those weathervanes. But—did you help someone *else* take them?"

"No!" yelped Ed. "What? *Me?* Listen, jerk! Guys help *me* on a stunt like that. I mean, Ed Grieg is either in charge or he doesn't touch it at all!"

McGurk took a deep breath.

"Okay. Fine. So—" McGurk had been pacing about. Suddenly he swung around and bent to Ed. *"Did you take them back?* The ones that *have* been taken back so far?"

Ed frowned.

"No, I did not," he said quietly.

Mari's face was very still. Her eyes seemed tighter shut.

"All right," said McGurk. "So did you *help* anyone take them back?"

Ed started up again.

"Listen! What *is* this? I just told you—"

"Did you *help* anyone take them back?" McGurk repeated.

Ed glared, then sat back.

"No . . . of *course* I didn't! Anyway, are *you* gonna help *me* or not?"

Mari had opened her eyes and was looking at McGurk.

"We'll see," he said. "I—" Then he caught Mari's look and the very faint nod. "Sure! We'll help you, Ed. But—one final question." (Mari quickly turned back to Ed, closing her eyes.) "Do you know who *did* take them?"

Ed sneered.

"What kind of fink do you take me for, McGurk? Do you think I'd tell you if I did know?"

"But—"

"No!" Ed got up and stalked to the door. "And that's flat!"

Then he flung the door open again and left.

"Well, Officer Yoshimura?" said McGurk.

"He was telling truth when he said he didn't take

them. He was also telling truth when he said he didn't help anyone else take them."

"How about helping to take them *back*, Officer Yoshimura? Was he telling the truth *then*?"

Mari frowned.

"Well, I am not sure. Partly, yes."

"What's that supposed to mean?"

"Well—"

Mari looked lost for words. I tried to help her out.

"Like he didn't *physically* help to take them back, but he might have helped some other way? Like with advice?"

Mari nodded, shaking her bangs.

"Yes! Yes, Joey! Yes!"

McGurk nodded, too, but much more slowly.

"So how about when I asked him if he knew the perpetrator?"

"Then—then he told truth, too. Yes."

Mari didn't sound so sure.

"Oh?"

"Well—yes, Chief McGurk. It *was* true when he said he wouldn't tell you."

"Which means," said McGurk, "that he *could* know."

"And probably *does*," murmured Brains.

I glanced at Wanda, feeling sorry for her.

"It looks like it," I said.

"Oh, the fool!" groaned Wanda, the tears starting. "Sticking his neck out for some other dumb jerk! He'll go to jail! He'll be *ruined!*"

McGurk put a hand on her shoulder.

"Don't worry, Officer Grieg," he said. "We won't let *that* happen!"

McGurk meant that seriously, I'm sure. But that evening, something happened that made things look blacker than ever for Ed.

I was watching the national TV news. It seemed much like on most nights. The anchorman—the guy who always looks terribly tense—was introducing the usual string of heavy items: arms negotiations, the war in the Middle East, the hostage situation, big-city corruption in New York, and the next day's elections.

I wasn't paying much attention. But then I heard my father say, "Hello! He's going to end on a lighter note. You can tell by his face!"

So I looked up and, sure enough, the guy wasn't exactly breaking up, but that grim, tight look around the mouth had relaxed and his eyes had a twinkle.

"But while the election watchers are pondering whether the wind of change will sweep through the Senate tomorrow, residents of a certain town in the

Northeast are struggling with a wind-related problem of their own. . . ."

And—you've guessed it!

Up came the Case of the Wandering Weathervanes once more—basically the same as last night's local segment, but focusing mainly on the interview with Mr. Getzoff and the same angry warning from Lieutenant Kaspar. And this time the payoff joke was delivered by the national anchorman himself.

"Will the rest of the weathervanes be returned? Or have they been blown away forever? Stay tuned but—don't hold your breath!"

I guess to him, after all that world-shaking stuff, our town's problem must have seemed like comic relief.

But I couldn't help thinking about how Lieutenant Kaspar would be taking this news item.

Whoever got nailed for this crime or stunt couldn't hope to get off with a slap on the wrist *now*. I mean, McGurk had been mad enough when he thought that Mark Westover's article would make the Organization the laughingstock of the town. So how could we expect Lieutenant Kaspar to feel anything but *fury*, after the twinkly eyed TV news anchorman had just made our police department the laughingstock of the *nation*?

Coast to coast! North, South, East, and West!

The Private
9 Investigator

Although the next day was a holiday, because of the elections, McGurk was in a gloomy mood when we gathered in his basement. I think the previous night's TV news item had affected him just as badly as it must have affected Lieutenant Kaspar.

"That Mark Westover story in the *Gazette*," he said, frowning. "Anyone seen it yet?"

We shook our heads. He sighed.

"Maybe he won't be writing it, after all."

"I wouldn't count on it, McGurk," I said. "You saw how much work he was putting into it. All those notes. He won't be wasting *them*!"

"No," growled McGurk. "I guess not. Where's Officer Yoshimura?"

"Dentist," said Wanda. "McGurk, you said yesterday you'd do everything you could to—to—"

"To clear Ed—yeah!" McGurk nodded, still frowning. "Let's get out on the streets and see what we can find out."

Wanda's face brightened as we followed McGurk out. He was setting such a brisk, businesslike pace. But it soon became clear that what he was so anxious to find out had little to do with Ed.

"What are we coming *here* for?" said Brains, as we turned into Main Street.

"To see if we can have a word with Mark Westover," said McGurk.

"Why?" I asked.

"Can't you guess?" muttered Wanda. "All he's worried about is—"

"Hey! There he is!" said McGurk. "Come on! Let's catch him before he gets into his car!"

Mark Westover was standing with another guy outside the *Gazette* office. He looked impatient, glancing up and down the street, as the man talked to him. When he saw us, his face lit up.

"Oh, hi!" he sang out. He turned to the man. "Here are some more private detectives." Then, to McGurk. "I was just telling this gentleman about the weathervanes."

We stared. He couldn't have taken us more by

surprise. Number one: The faces of very few adults, if any, *ever* light up when they see McGurk coming. Number two: That one small word, "more"—some *more* private detectives—could only mean that the guy was the real professional thing!

McGurk was already focusing on the stranger— his eyes shining.

"Hi!" he said, sticking out his hand. "Pleased to meet you, sir!"

The guy ignored McGurk's hand. He didn't even seem to have seen *McGurk*. He was looking at Mark Westover.

"You were telling me about the weathervanes. . . ."

He was a big man, taller even than Mark Westover, and much bulkier. He had a reddish brown face, crisscrossed with little purple veins, and small, pale blue, doll-like eyes. With his snub nose and broad mouth, he had a good face for smiling. In fact, there was a slight smile on it now. But those little eyes were hard and steady.

"Cop's eyes," McGurk said later. "You could tell at a glance."

Mark Westover was looking uneasy.

"Well, all I can tell you is that no more have been brought back. Just the eight I mentioned. It *is* a kid's stunt, I'm sure. But the police have over-

reacted, in my view. Kaspar has obviously scared the daylights out of the pranksters, and now the victims will be lucky if any more weathervanes *are* brought back. Voluntarily."

While the reporter was talking, we studied the newcomer. His clothes had an old-fashioned look. He wore a big gray hat with a fairly wide brim and one of those brown, loose hairy overcoats with leather buttons. The bottoms of his thick gray pants were wide but short—showing a lot of very pale gray sock between them and the big black shoes.

"Anyway," said Mark Westover, fumbling with the door handle of the car. "That's all I know. You'll be able to read about it in full detail tonight. When my article appears."

McGurk winced.

"Hey, yes, Mr. Westover! I was going to ask you about that."

The reporter grinned.

"Oh, don't worry, McGurk! Now that the affair has taken a different turn, we had to cut out some of the lighter trimmings. *His* weathervane won't be mentioned now," he said, glancing at Brains.

McGurk positively *glowed* with relief.

"Gee, thanks!"

"Don't thank *me*," said Mark Westover. "Thank the police and the TV people for making such a big deal out of it. Now, if you'll excuse me, I have an election to cover."

As the car rolled away, the stranger looked at us. His smile broadened some but the eyes stayed small and shrewd and watchful.

"So you're private investigators, too, eh? My name's Truswell, Bob Truswell. Any—"

"And mine's—"

"McGurk. Yes. Any leads so far?"

McGurk was delighted to have his name so readily noted. He thrust out his ID card.

"There's my ID, sir. These are my assistants: Officer Rockaway, Officer Grieg . . ."

As McGurk went through the roll call, the man gave each of us one quick, hard glance—flick! flick! flick! flick!

Then he handed back the card.

"Do *you* have one, sir?" said McGurk, hardly able to contain his eagerness to feast his eyes on a real private investigator's ID card.

"Of course," said the man, not making the slightest attempt to get it out. "You haven't answered my question. Any leads?"

"Well—"

McGurk blinked; his freckles squirmed. The man's eyes stayed small and steady.

"Any *theories* then?"

That loosened McGurk up.

"Oh, yes, sure! It's either a student stunt that went wrong—or—"

McGurk broke off and chewed uncertainly at his lower lip.

"Or?"

McGurk shrugged. Then he put on his savvy, man-to-man expression.

"Well, *you* know how it is, Mr. Truswell—"

"No. I don't know how it is, McGurk. Tell me."

"Well, I mean—well—it could have been staged

to *look* like a student stunt. To cover up the real motive."

Wanda gasped. Brains pushed his glasses farther back on his nose and frowned. Mr. Truswell looked *very* interested now.

"What real motive?"

"Like one of those weathervanes was really worth a fortune," said McGurk. "And some wealthy collector hired someone to swipe it but take a whole bunch more, to make it look like a kid's stunt." That deep, knowing, cunning look had come back to McGurk's face. "Wealthy collectors do operate like that. As of course you know, sir."

The man was nodding slowly.

"That's a very interesting theory, McGurk," he said. "As a matter of fact . . ." He paused, then shrugged. "I myself have been hired by someone whose valuable weathervane has been taken."

"*Really*, sir?"

"Yes," said the guy. "Except you could hardly call a few thousand dollars a fortune, these days. But it was also of great sentimental value, I guess."

"Gee!" said McGurk. "Which was the one *you've* been hired to—?"

"Ah-ah!" The man wagged a large finger in front of McGurk's face. "You should know better than to ask that, McGurk! We private investigators *never* disclose the names of clients. Anyway, if you hear anything that might point to who's responsible for taking these things, maybe you'll call me at"—he dug into a pocket and brought out a scrap of paper— "this number."

"Sure!" said McGurk, reaching out.

But Mr. Truswell kept hold of the paper and read out the number instead.

"That's a local number," I murmured, jotting it down.

The man waited only long enough to hear me read it back, then pulled his hat farther over his eyes and sauntered away without another word.

On the way back, we spent some time wondering which weathervane it was that he'd been asked to retrieve—the $3,000 Gabriel Blowing Horn or some other similarly expensive one. At least, Wanda, Willie, Brains, and I did. McGurk said nothing, too busy making *his* eyes go little and hard, and flicking them this way and that.

Then Wanda turned on him.

"What's wrong, McGurk? Lost your tongue? You found it soon enough back there. Showing off. Telling a complete stranger about your hunch before telling *us*!"

"Yeah!" we said. And, "She's right!" And, "How about that, McGurk?"

But he ducked that one.

"Forget it!" he said. "That was only a backup theory. We haven't worked our way through the main one yet. Let's go see if Mealy Oates is home."

10 Mealy Digs a Trench

On the way to Mealy Oates's house, Wanda said, "Shouldn't we wait until Mari gets back?"

"Why?" said McGurk.

"To see if Mealy lies when we question him."

"Who says we're going to do that?" said McGurk. "I'm hoping he *isn't* home."

"Oh?" I said. "Why are you hoping *that*, McGurk?"

"Because I want to do what all good detectives *should* do at this stage. I want to take a look around the suspect's premises. At least around his yard and maybe in the garage."

That silenced us. It made sense. Kind of.

Mealy's house was on Hickory Avenue, near the

ranch house where the Hounds Chasing Fox weathervane had been swiped.

"It's certainly conveniently located," I said, as we paused at the end of the driveway.

"Huh?"

McGurk was studying the house. It was a regular two-story building, with a separate garage. The garage door was shut, and there was no car in the driveway.

"I mean convenient according to your theory," I said. "Well placed for Mealy to slip out in the dark Saturday and start replacing those eight."

McGurk nodded. "Yeah, but we didn't have to come here to check on *that*. . . . It looks like no one's at home," he added. "But there's only one way to find out."

We followed him up the driveway. The front yard was very tidy. Most of the fallen leaves had been swept up and bagged, with a neat double row of plump black garbage sacks all around the foundations.

"That's a very dangerous practice," said Brains.

"What is?" said McGurk.

"Putting sacks of leaves around a house for extra insulation," said Brains. "It could be a fire hazard."

McGurk glared. "What *are* we, Officer Bellingham? A team of detectives hot on the trail of a

perpetrator? Or a bunch of fire marshals?"

Then he went up to the front door and rang the
bell.

There was no response.

He rang again.

"What will you say if someone comes?" Wanda
whispered.

McGurk shrugged. "I'll think of something," he
muttered.

"We could say we've come to point out the fire
hazard," said Brains. "We—"

"Officer Bellingham!" growled McGurk, pressing

the bell push a third time. "One more word about fire hazards and—"

He broke off.

"There *is* someone home!" Willie whispered. "Someone out in back!"

"Yeah!" murmured McGurk, his eyes beginning to gleam. "Someone *digging*!" He began to move, very slowly. "Follow me, men!" he whispered.

Between the garage and the house, there was a narrow walkway with evergreen bushes on either side. We took advantage of that cover, walking very slowly and softly. When McGurk reached the corner, he stopped and lifted his hand, peering cautiously. We bunched up behind him, peering also. I began to get goose bumps.

The digging noise was coming from behind a tall burlap screen. It reminded me of a scene from the movies—where the police had to dig up a buried corpse.

Then I realized that the burlap wasn't really that kind of screen at all. It had been set up around a small tree for protection against winter frosts.

"*Someone's* a keen gardener here," whispered Wanda.

McGurk began to inch forward until he was able to peek around the edge of the screen.

He turned, his face glowing.

"It's—Mea-ly!" he mouthed. "Dig-ging. Dig-ging—a—*hole!*"

We stared.

Mealy had his back to us, grunting with every stab of the spade. There was also a gardening fork stuck in the grass at the side of the long trench he was working on. Beyond him was another row of leaf sacks, this time ranged along the fence.

"Is—is he burying the weathervanes?" Willie whispered.

I couldn't see any sign of them, but the trench sure looked long enough to take the whole dozen or so that were still missing. Most of it seemed to have been filled in, too, with the fresh earth in brimming black lumps.

"Maybe he already *has* buried them," I whispered.

McGurk waved us quiet.

Mealy was taking a breather, leaning on the spade.

We kept very still.

When I said earlier that Mealy was only three-fourths the size of Ed Grieg, I didn't mean that he was a shrimp. He was still taller than any of *us*, and, judging from the way he'd been digging, he was certainly no weakling. So the situation could get very ugly if—

Then Willie made that "if" a reality.

He sneezed.

And with *his* nose, a sneeze from Willie is something else!

Mealy was as agile as I'd feared. He had to be, to jump that far in the air from a standing start.

His eyes popped as he stared at us. There was no telling what he might have done next if Wanda hadn't stepped forward, smiled, and said,

"Hi, Kevin!" She was careful to use Mealy's real name.

"Oh—hi, Wanda!" said Mealy, blinking at her and plucking at the feeble strands of his mustache. "Do you have a message from Ed?"

Wanda's *instincts* had been right, anyway. But beyond that she wasn't sure how to proceed.

Someone was, though. Quick as a cat pouncing on a mouse, McGurk said, "Yes! Ed's been having trouble with *his* VW. He wants to know if he can borrow your owner's manual."

Mealy's face brightened.

"Sure!" he said. "I'll get it now. Come on!"

As he rolled the garage door up and over, Wanda murmured in my ear, "Ed'll be *furious* when he finds out we used his name like this!"

I nodded. Just then, though, I was too busy looking into the garage to worry about that. I glanced to see if McGurk was also making the best of the opportunity and was surprised to see he wasn't around. Then I continued my inspection, while Mealy fumbled around inside the car.

There was a folded stepladder leaning against the back wall. And this garage wasn't as tidy as the Griegs'. There were some fairly large piles of junk along the sides. Mealy soon emerged, holding out the booklet to Wanda, but there'd been enough time for me to see that *some* weathervanes could have been stashed away in there. A dozen or more, though—I wasn't sure. McGurk might have been able to judge it better, but—where was he, the jerk, just when he was needed? Could it be that—?

Suddenly, I realized what had kept him. I started talking in a loud voice as we followed Mealy back along the walkway.

"I didn't know you were such a keen gardener, Kevin. I'm sorry we interrupted your—"

As we went back around the burlapped tree, McGurk had just finished replacing the garden fork. He shot me a look of appreciation and said,

"Yeah. I guess we interrupted your digging, Kevin. What *is* this strip, anyway?"

Mealy frowned.

"Uh—well—it's a trench. You know. For asparagus. Yeah. Asparagus. Mom's favorite."

It didn't require Mari to detect that jittery lack of conviction. Even Willie sniffed suspiciously, while McGurk was positively beady-eyed. Wanda frowned.

"But you can't plant asparagus at this time of the year. The frost will—"

"Yeah! Ah! Sure!" I thought Mealy was going to pluck that mustache right out in his nervousness. "The frost! Yeah. No! I mean—oh, no—no, no, *no*, Wanda!" His smile was twitchy. "No! I don't intend planting them *now*! Ha! But if you dig *now*, late fall, and turn the soil over, the winter frost and snow and ice and stuff—why, it'll break the clods up good and crumbly. So—well—come spring—it'll be *perfect!*"

Wanda was nodding.

"Well—yes . . ."

"Anyway," said McGurk, "we won't hold you up any more. It's been nice talking to you."

When we were back on the street, I said, "You think he's been burying the evidence, McGurk?"

McGurk nodded. "Well, it *would* be a good place."

"But he was only turning it over," said Brains. "I mean, he wasn't filling in a hole, as far as I could see."

"I didn't say he'd buried it *yet*, Officer Bellingham! In fact I *know* he hasn't, because—"

"You jabbed that fork all along the trench, right, McGurk?" I said. "While we went to the garage?"

"Yes," he said. "And I didn't strike any metal object. He was probably getting ready to bury the weathervanes, sure! But"—McGurk's face clouded—"he won't now. Not there."

"They must be around someplace, though," said Wanda. "In some temporary hiding place."

"Maybe," McGurk murmured. "How about the garage?"

I frowned.

"I don't know. There *were* places in there, but not for a whole bunch."

"Joey's right," said Brains.

"And then there are his parents," said Wanda. "They use the garage, too. He'd never risk it."

"So where *would* someone stash fourteen or fifteen weathervanes?" McGurk said, looking absolutely baffled. "Knowing that the heat's on and the police could stop by any—uh-oh!"

Some heavy drops of rain had started to fall.

"It's time for lunch, anyway," McGurk grunted, breaking into a run.

And that put an end to the morning's investigations.

In fact, the rain put an end to our investigations for the rest of the day, but McGurk made sure it wasn't a complete washout. Not as far as I was concerned, anyway.

"I want you to draw a street map, Officer Rockaway," he said, when he called me up midafternoon. "I want you to make it good and clear, showing the locations where those eight weathervanes turned up, Saturday night. In relation to Mealy's house."

"Sure!" I said. "But why?"

"I want it to be good and clear when we confront the suspect with it and see how he reacts."

"But don't you think we ought to find some *hard* evidence first?" I said. "Like the weathervanes that *haven't* shown up yet?"

Heavy sigh at the other end. Then:

"That won't be long. If it wasn't for the rain we'd be closing in on them now."

"You mean you *know* where they're stashed?" I said.

Another pause.

"Well, no. . . . But I do have some ideas."

"Would you like to share those ideas?" I said.

Yet another pause, followed by:

"Uh—not now. I *could* be wrong, and—"

"You've no more idea than *I* have, McGurk."

"Officer Rockaway!" he growled. "Just get on with the map, okay?"

I didn't argue anymore and I did get on with the map. Here is a copy:

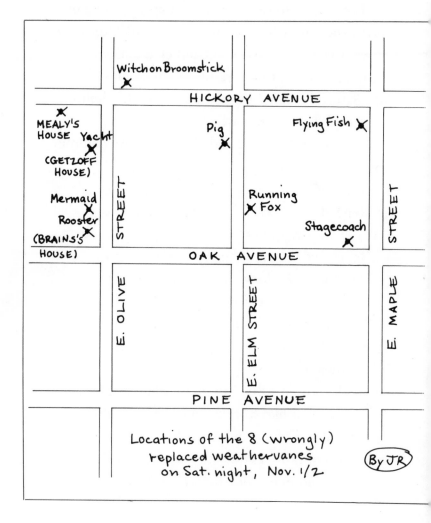

Locations of the 8 (wrongly) replaced weathervanes on Sat. night, Nov. 1/2

By JR

I was very proud of that map, especially for having thought to include those extra stretches of Olive, Elm, and Maple to emphasize the narrowness of the area where the eight weathervanes reappeared. I could hardly wait to get to school the next morning and show it to the others.

Then Wanda blew it clear out of my mind.

"Hi, Wanda!" I said, when Willie and I caught up with her in the school yard. "Did McGurk call *you* yesterday aft—?"

My voice trailed off. She looked so upset. Mari, next to her, looked grave and shook her head to warn me.

"Hey!" I said. "What's wrong? *Did* Mealy call up and ask Ed if that VW manual would be useful?"

To our horror, she burst into tears, dipping her head to hide them.

"Oh, boy!" I murmured. "Mealy did call, huh? And was Ed *that* mad?"

Wanda lifted her head and, with what must have been a tremendous effort, checked her tears.

"I—I don't know, Joey," she said. "I don't even know if Mealy did call him. Someone—*someone* did, that's for sure!"

"Oh?" I said. "But—"

"And Ed went out and said—said he had to meet

someone downtown. Said he—he might be late. . . ."

There was a long pause. Wanda seemed to be fighting to keep control.

"So?" Willie said, softly. "Uh—was he late?"

"Yes. I mean no. I mean"—Wanda's voice broke into a wail—"he didn't come back at *all*! He's gone! Vanished! Without packing a bag, leaving a message, getting in touch again—any-any-*anything*!"

11 Mr. Truswell Stops By

When we met down in McGurk's basement that afternoon, Wanda was able to tell us more details. Here are the main facts about Ed's disappearance:

1. He'd taken his car.

2. *But*—he'd taken no spare clothes, toilet things, or other personal belongings, as far as the family could tell.

3. Ed had, very occasionally, taken off like this before. Usually only for a couple of days, at vacation time. Like to go on a last-minute skiing trip. That kind of thing.

4. *But*—this time he'd said he'd be back later in the evening—and that was what worried Wanda and her mother. (Not so much her father, who was

treating this as yet another case of teenage irresponsibility.)

5. The police—besides not taking the matter seriously enough in itself—also seemed to regard it as a sign of Ed's guilt over the weathervane caper.

("How do you know that?" McGurk had asked.

Wanda shrugged. "I was listening on the extension when Mom called them this morning, and I could sense it in the desk sergeant's voice."

"Huh!" McGurk replied. "It could have been your imagination. Now, if Officer Yoshimura had heard his voice and *she'd* sensed it, that would be something else.")

6. *But*—there was a similar situation in our own files.

"Simon Emmet," I reminded Wanda and the others. "The Case of the Nervous Newsboy. *He* ran away when he was suspected of something he hadn't done."

"Sure!" said Wanda. "But Ed isn't like that. Ed isn't the nervous type. *He* wouldn't run away, guilty or—or not guilty."

She didn't sound so sure.

"Anyway, Ed *isn't* guilty," McGurk said.

"Thanks, McGurk!" said Wanda, shooting him a grateful glance.

Brains was frowning.

"But why *would* Ed take off like that?" he said. "Before this weathervane thing is cleared up? He must have known it would make him *look* guilty."

"Maybe he did it as a protest," said Wanda. "To remind the police that there are more important things than student pranks. Who knows?"

"Yeah, who knows?" murmured McGurk. "But our job right now, men, is to nail the real perpetrator. Maybe when we—"

There was a loud knock on the outer door.

"See who it is, Officer Sandowsky," McGurk said. "It could even be Ed himself, come to—"

That's when Willie opened the door to reveal the tall, bulky figure of—no, not Ed, but Mr. Truswell.

"Hi!" he said, standing in the doorway. "I rang the front doorbell, but no one answered." His little eyes flicked this way and that. "Nice place you've got here, McGurk."

McGurk was already on his feet, his face squirming with pleasure at this compliment.

"Yeah—thanks! Come in and take a seat," he said, waving to Willie's chair.

The man took one step inside but came no farther. He seemed to prefer to stand by the open door. He tipped his hat farther back on his head.

"Any leads yet?" he said.

"Uh—no, sir," said McGurk. "Have you?"

The man shook his head.

"I've been thinking about your theories, McGurk. Somehow I think we can rule out the wealthy collector coverup one."

"Yes, sir?"

"Yes. One of the things you have to learn, McGurk, is to follow up on the simplest, most obvious theory first. In this case, the kids' prank theory."

McGurk nodded.

"Yes! That's exactly what I've been telling my officers, right, men?"

There was some doubtful murmuring at this, but the man paid it no attention. Still looking at McGurk, he said,

"So? Any idea which kid might have done it?"

McGurk smiled uneasily.

"Well, there's one prime suspect that everyone thought of, but—"

"But he didn't do it!" said Wanda. "And—and it's a rotten shame—it's—"

"Easy, Officer Grieg!"

"I don't care!" said Wanda. "He's my brother, and now he's—he's—"

She broke off, biting her lip.

The man was looking at her, his eyes smaller than ever.

"That'll be the kid called Ed Grieg, right? I've been hearing his name mentioned a lot."

"Yes, sir," said Wanda. "And he's innocent! We *all* know he's innocent. . . ." She looked around, then stamped her foot. "Well, *don't* we?"

"Sure!"

"Of course!"

"You bet!"

"Well—yeah!"

The man flicked a glance at each of us as we responded. The only one who didn't say anything— just nodded her head—was Mari. She had her eyes shut tight.

The detective frowned slightly.

"Who's she?"

"Oh—uh—Officer Yoshimura, sir. She wasn't with us yesterday, but—"

The man interrupted McGurk.

"So who else might it have been if it wasn't the Grieg kid? Some buddy of his, maybe?"

McGurk reddened.

"Maybe. But—uh—well—none of the other high-school kids have what it takes."

We all stared at McGurk. The man's little eyes were like tiny blue beads now.

"You sure you're leveling with me, McGurk?"

McGurk's face was on fire.

"Well, *you* know how it is, sir!" His smile squirmed. "A good private investigator doesn't disclose the names of his suspects until he has some real evidence. Like—like he doesn't disclose the name of a client."

The man's shoulders stiffened. Then his smile broadened a little.

"Touché!" he murmured. "I reckon I asked for that one, sport! Anyway, I take it you haven't got any real evidence yet?"

"No, sir," said McGurk. "But if we do, we'll let you know."

"Hmm. Good. You have my number?"

"Yes, Mr. Truswell," I said.

The man nodded, turned, and left, with a grunted good-bye. We crowded onto the basement steps and watched him walk down the driveway. There was a silver gray car parked on the street. He got into it, backed a little way into the driveway, and drove off.

McGurk turned to Mari, as soon as we'd resumed our places around the table.

"I noticed your eyes were closed, Officer Yoshimura. Was *he* telling any lies?"

Mari shook her head slowly.

"I am sorry, Chief McGurk. But he was asking questions, not answering them. Perhaps if you had asked him—"

"Yeah, yeah!" McGurk looked miffed. Then he shrugged. "Forget it, anyway. He wouldn't have come to us if he *had* known anything."

"There was one thing," Mari said quietly.

"Oh?"

"Yes," she said, her eyes lowered. "Something that puzzled me."

Her lips began moving silently, like she was repeating something to herself.

"What? *What* puzzled you, Officer Yoshimura?"

She blinked at McGurk.

"You told me he was true private investigator."

"Sure! So?"

"So, don't real private detectives as well as police detectives—don't they have to be American citizens?"

"Well, sure," said McGurk. Then he laughed.

"Hey, Officer Yoshimura, don't worry about *that*! You may not be an American citizen yet, but if *I* say you can be a member of the McGurk Organization, you can!"

"No, no, Chief McGurk! What puzzles me is that that man—he is *not* an American!"

McGurk gaped.

"You—you could have fooled *me*!" he said. "How about you guys?"

We shook our heads. Then:

"I reckon I asked for that one, sport!"

Wanda gave a little scream. Willie nearly jumped out of his chair. The rest of us gasped and looked over our shoulders.

It was just as if the guy had crept back into the room!

Then we all turned to Mari, who was saying it again, head bent over the table, eyes closed, giving a perfect imitation of that voice.

She sighed and looked up.

"Yes. I think he is Australian. Or maybe Englishman. It came out most clearly when he said those words."

McGurk's eyes gleamed.

"Say it again, Officer Yoshimura. Like him. Only slower."

She did. And this time I thought I, too, could

detect something not American in the way he/she said "sport." More like "spoat." And there was a hint of "ah-sked" in that "asked."

Then I shook my head.

"Maybe you're right, Mari," I said. "Could be he *is* an Australian or an Englishman—by birth. But he could be a *naturalized* American. A citizen."

Mari nodded.

"I see," she said. "Well, I thought I should mention it. I am sorry, Chief McGurk, if—"

"Forget it, Officer Yoshimura! You did good! Anyway," McGurk continued, getting up, "let's not waste any more time on *that*. Let's pay Mealy Oates another visit. See if Ed's disappearance has shaken him up some."

"Good! He's home," said McGurk.

Mealy's car was in the driveway. The afternoon sun was shining on the still-wet grass and picking out little blobs of water on the garbage bags.

"If he put the leaves in dry, it would still be a fire hazard," said Brains, as we walked up the driveway. "I just can't understand—"

"Officer Bellingham!" growled McGurk.

Brains fell silent. McGurk rang the bell. Again there was no response. This time there was no sound of digging, either.

"Maybe he's doing some other garden job," said Wanda.

But Mealy wasn't out in the back. The garden fork was still stuck in the grass, but there was no sign of the spade. The black strip of upturned soil looked the same, too, except that now it was very wet.

McGurk picked up the fork and gave the strip a few thoughtful jabs.

"Hey! Should you be doing that, McGurk?" Willie said. "I mean, if he sees you—"

"He's gone out, Officer Sandowsky. So how can he see me?"

"Oh, no, he hasn't!" said Willie, with a confident sniff.

"Huh?" McGurk started peering every which way. "I don't see him."

"No. Me either," said Willie. "But I can smell him. Bay rum."

"Rum?"

"*Bay* rum. Some folks put it on their hair. It makes it grow springier."

"So Mealy uses it, huh?" McGurk sniffed. "Are you *sure* you can smell it?"

"Sure!" said Willie. "I noticed it yesterday. It was very strong then. I guess he uses it on that mustache thing."

"So—where's it coming from?" said McGurk, whispering now.

"Over here, I think," said Willie, walking toward the house, sniffing. "Yeah. He's in there."

He pointed to one of the basement windows. It was impossible to see anything beyond the screen except the window itself, which was open a crack.

"You sure?"

"Sure!" said Willie.

That was enough for McGurk. "Officer Yoshimura, you listen carefully to this." He turned back to the window. "Hey, Mealy! Are you there?"

There was no reply, but Willie was nodding positively.

"Uh—Kevin"—now McGurk's voice was softer— "it's okay. We only want to ask you a few questions."

No reply.

"About those weathervanes, Kevin," McGurk continued. "It'll be better for you to talk to us first, rather than the cops."

I was sure I heard the sound of someone moving at the mention of cops. McGurk must have heard it, too.

"Kevin, we know you're—"

"Oh, come out of the way!" Wanda looked mad as she pushed in front of McGurk. "Listen to me, you creep, you jerk!" she snarled. "My brother is in big trouble because of you, you coward, you . . ."

She went on like that nonstop, getting madder and louder by the second. In one way it was laughable—McGurk and Wanda talking to what looked like a blank window, one wheedling, one yelling, like they were grilling a *house*, for pete's sake!

Then it ended abruptly with the sound of a car door being shut.

No. It was not the suspect making a getaway. It was the suspect's mother, just home from work.

"What's going on?" she said, turning the corner.

She was a tall, frowning woman, dressed in a black

suit and carrying a briefcase. I remembered she worked in a bank as an assistant manager.

"Uh—we—we were just having a word with Kevin, ma'am," said McGurk.

"Kevin?"

Mrs. Oates raised her eyebrows, looking around.

"He's in there!" said Wanda, disdainfully.

Then the window spoke at last.

"Hi, Mom! I was telling these kids to go away. They're trespassing."

Mrs. Oates stared at us.

"Really?"

"No, ma'am," said McGurk. "We only wanted to ask him something. But it'll keep. . . . Come on, men!"

"Very interesting!" murmured Brains, when we hit the street.

"Oh?" said McGurk.

"Yes. I haven't seen Mrs. Oates in a long time. I'd forgotten how she looked."

"So?"

Brains shrugged.

"So she certainly doesn't look the type to try to save on fuel bills by insulating the house with sacks of leaves. A fire hazard—"

"Officer Bellingham!" growled McGurk. "One more word about that and *you're* fired! Okay?"

"Sorry!" mumbled Brains.

"Anyway," said McGurk, "Mealy told us *one* thing."

"What?" said Wanda.

"That those weathervanes must be hidden someplace close by. Probably in a hole which he's covered with grass again. Or in a hollow tree. Someplace like that."

"Oh?" I said.

"Yeah. Why else would he be so anxious to keep an eye on us, when he could have been upstairs, watching TV or something?"

"So what do we do now?" said Willie.

"So tomorrow we pay him another visit," said McGurk. "Earlier in the afternoon. When his mom won't be able to butt in."

"And then what?" said Wanda.

"Then we play Hotter and Colder with him."

"Chief McGurk?" said Mari.

"Like the game," McGurk explained. "We prowl *slowly* around the yard, inspecting this and that, and when we start getting closer to wherever the stash is—when we're really hot—*then* he'll come out and talk to us. You'll see!"

12 Another Disappearance

That was on Wednesday afternoon. But McGurk didn't get to make that visit on Thursday, because two important new developments turned up.

For several days, the direction of the case had kept veering: from fairly mild to fairly serious, from fairly clear to fairly cloudy. After Thursday morning, it stayed in one direction only: dark and deadly dangerous.

When we were in the thick of this new murkiness and in danger of losing our bearings, McGurk had me type out a timetable of all the different events and developments. "To see if there's some kind of thread running through it," he explained.

Well, here's a copy of the first part. Even without Thursday's developments, there was a kind of thread—if only we'd known what to look for.

Weathervanes Case - Timetable

FRI/SAT NIGHT OCT. 31/NOV. 1
  Weathervanes disappear all over town.

SAT. NOV. 1 MORNING
  Police called in. McGurk Organization starts investigating.
          AFTERNOON
  McGurk Organization start interview with Ed Grieg.
  (Ed slips out back way.)

SAT/SUN NIGHT
  8 weathervanes reappear (at wrong houses, our neighborhood.)

SUN. MORNING
  McGurk O. interviews Ed Grieg (in bed).
  Ed denies complicity but receives call from Mealy Oates.

SUN. AFTERNOON
  Ed offers fingerprints to police.

SUN. EVENING
  Weathervane story on local TV news, including interviews with
  Mr. Getzoff and Lt. Kaspar.

MON. AFTERNOON
  Ed comes to McGurk O. seeking information. (Worried?).
  Mari thinks Ed telling truth about not having hand in
  weathervane caper, but might have given advice to real
  perpetrator about returning them.

MON. EVENING
  Weathervane story on national TV, including interviews with
  Mr. Getzoff and Lt. Kaspar.

TUE. MORNING
  McGurk O. talk to Mark Westover and Bob Truswell
  (private investigator).
  McGurk O. interviews Mealy Oates.

TUE. EVENING
  Ed Grieg receives phone call (around 9:00 P.M.), goes out
  in car--and disappears.

WED. MORNING
  No news of ED

WED. AFTERNOON
  Mr. Truswell visits us, seeking info. about likely perpetrators.
  McGurk stalls him. McGurk O. try to interview Mealy. He hides
  in basement.

So what were the new developments on Thursday?

We heard about the first from Wanda, in school. Ed's car had been found. It had been spotted by a neighbor, late the previous evening, in a parking garage near the train station. It had been left in the long-stay section.

Again the police didn't regard it as alarming.

"Just another piece of evidence that Ed has gone off on some teenage jaunt, probably by train," said Wanda, looking both sad and mad. "All they could say was, 'We can't post him as a missing person until forty-eight hours have elapsed.' "

"Which is tonight," said McGurk.

"Which may be too late!" snapped Wanda.

The second development came midafternoon. Once again, it was Brains who brought the news. We were in McGurk's basement, getting ready to visit Mealy. Then Brains burst in.

"Hey! There's been another disappearance!"

"Who?" said McGurk.

"Mr. Getzoff!" said Brains.

"When?"

"Last night. After dinner. Mrs. Getzoff was telling Mom this morning. She was very upset. Especially"—Brains glanced uneasily at Wanda—"especially when the cops didn't seem to take it

seriously. Just another domestic problem."

"Never mind that stuff, Officer Bellingham. Did *he* go in his car? Did *he* take any belongings? Did *he* say where he was going?"

Brains filled us in with those details he knew about.

Yes. Mr. Getzoff had taken his car.

No. He hadn't taken any belongings.

No. He hadn't said where he was going.

"He *had* been kind of worried, though," said Brains. "Ever since Tuesday afternoon. That's what Mrs. Getzoff told Mom. And she even said something about how it seemed to be connected with—"

Brains hesitated.

"With *what*?" said McGurk.

"With Ed Grieg."

"*What*?"

This time it was Wanda who yelled the word.

"Well—with Ed's disappearance. She said it seemed to make Mr. Getzoff even more worried. Look, I'm only telling you what Mom told me."

"That's okay, Officer Bellingham," said McGurk. "Officer Grieg, sit down. Let him tell us what else he learned."

Brains wiped his forehead.

"Well, nothing. Oh, yeah—except there was something about a phone call. Just before he took off. Only in *his* case *he* made the call."

McGurk stood up, face flushed, eyes gleaming.

"Something tells me there's a kind of link here. But we need more information. Come on!"

"Where?" I asked, as we followed him out.

"To Mrs. Getzoff," he said.

"Hey!" said Wanda. "She must be very upset. We can't just—"

"So *you're* upset, too, aren't you?" said McGurk. "But that doesn't stop you from talking about it, does it? Especially to someone who might be able to help!"

Wanda quickened her pace, matching McGurk stride for stride.

Personally, I didn't feel comfortable about this. But—what do you know?—McGurk's instincts must have been absolutely right. When Mrs. Getzoff opened the door, she was pale and red-eyed and seemed somehow shrunken. But she welcomed us with a kind of hungry eagerness.

"Wanda Grieg!" she said. "I was just thinking about your poor mother. Any news?"

Wanda shook her head.

"Only that we've found his car. In the—"

"Come in! All of you! Please!" She glanced over our heads up and down the street, half-hopeful, half-anxious. "Come through into the kitchen. I was just having a cup of coffee."

It looked more like a gift shop than a kitchen—what with the cuckoo clock and dozens of fancy mugs and jugs and shiny brass vases and urns and pans all over the place. But soon we were sitting in front of glasses of milk and plates of cookies, while Mrs. Getzoff continued to question Wanda. When Wanda said how annoyed she and her mother were at the police for still regarding it as a teenage escapade, Mrs. Getzoff nodded.

"I know! I know! They were the same when I reported Stanley's disappearance." She sniffed. "Suggesting it was maybe because we'd had a fight, of all things!"

"Uh—" McGurk cleared his throat. I wondered if he was going to say, "And *did* you have a fight?" But he took a bite out of his cookie instead, though he still kept his eyes on her.

She sighed and poured herself some more coffee.

"These are nice tumblers," Wanda murmured.

They were each made of a different colored glass.

We all looked at our tumblers. Except McGurk, who was still watching Mrs. Getzoff's face.

"Thank you," she said. "We got them in Italy. We always bring souvenirs back from our vacations." Her eyes filled up. She brushed the back of her hand across them and waved at the vases and pans and clock and stuff.

"We got that clock in Switzerland . . . and those came from Montreal . . . and—"

That's when McGurk spoke.

"The weathervane. That was a souvenir, too, wasn't it, ma'am?"

She sighed again.

"Yes. That came from Connecticut. Near Mystic Seaport."

She fell silent.

Mari had been frowning. Then:

"Whales," she said quietly, nodding.

Mrs. Getzoff looked at her.

"No, no—Connecticut. The vase with the daffodil pattern—*that* came from Wales."

Mari blinked.

"I'm sorry. I meant whales in the sea, not Wales the country. In August *I* went to Mystic with my parents. There is a museum—"

"Officer Yoshimura, Mrs. Getzoff was telling us about the weathervane!"

McGurk looked annoyed.

"I know, Chief McGurk. But then, after going to

whaling museum we went on to another town nearby, where there is submarine museum."

"That's right," said Mrs. Getzoff. "At Groton. In fact, the man we bought the weathervane from had once worked at the nuclear submarine plant there. Which is why so many of his weathervanes were shaped like submarines, I guess.

"Yours was the *Nautilus*," said Brains, dunking his cookie like *it* was a sub. "The first nuclear—"

He stopped. His cookie crash-dived, slopping some milk. McGurk had given him a terribly dirty look and a sharp nudge. McGurk turned and said,

"I'm sorry, ma'am. These guys get carried away sometimes. You were telling us about buying the weathervane. Wasn't the guy killed, soon afterward?"

"Yes. I—I think Stanley mentioned it on television. And I'm beginning to believe that that weathervane really *was* jinxed."

Mrs. Getzoff suppressed a shudder. I wondered if McGurk had stepped out of line, mentioning something as gruesome as the man's sudden death, but she seemed glad of the chance to talk about it.

She told us what we'd heard before. About the store owner's nervousness, his locking the door, and then his death in the car a short time later, followed by the burglary at his store.

"It seems he was in a hurry to leave," said McGurk.

"Yes." Mrs. Getzoff was staring into her cup, her forehead giving little twitches, like she was trying to recall something that puzzled her. "But he didn't rush *us* out. In fact, he even spent time engraving it."

"Engraving the weathervane?" asked McGurk.

"Yes. He said each one he sold had to be personally initialed by him and engraved with its own special catalog number. He took it in back and kept us waiting about ten minutes."

McGurk had taken a bite out of his fourth cookie, just after he'd asked the question, but he didn't get to chew it until Mrs. Getzoff had finished her answer. Wanda took up the questioning.

"Brains—uh—Gerald says Mr. Getzoff had been worried about Ed, Mrs. Getzoff. . . ."

The woman nodded.

"Well—yes. He was."

"Did he think Ed had had anything to do with taking the weathervanes?" asked McGurk.

Mrs. Getzoff nodded again.

"Yes—but only the way most people thought it was Ed. Only because of his track record." She glanced apologetically at Wanda. "That's what he told the man, anyway."

"What man?" said McGurk. "The TV interviewer?"

"No—I don't think he mentioned it to *him*. This was the detective."

"The *private* detective?" said McGurk.

"Yes. Mr. Trustwell, I think his name was."

"When was this, ma'am?"

"Tuesday afternoon. I remember that because it was Tuesday dinnertime when I realized Stanley was upset. And when I asked him what it was, he said he'd been wrong to mention Ed's name, just on hearsay. That—that it wasn't fair."

"No," said Wanda.

Mrs. Getzoff blinked.

"Then when he heard about your brother's disappearance, he became more than just upset. He became very depressed, broody."

"When was that, ma'am?"

"Oh, sometime on Wednesday—yesterday." She smiled faintly, shaking her head. "Heavens! It seems years ago!"

"Was Mr. Getzoff still depressed when he made the phone call?" asked McGurk.

"Yes. Very. He'd hardly spoken a word to me all day."

"Was—was the call *about* Ed, Mrs. Getzoff?" Wanda murmured.

"I don't know," said Mrs. Getzoff. "I wasn't listening. I—I wish I had been." She suddenly frowned at McGurk. "Anyway, why are you asking all these questions?"

McGurk squirmed.

"Oh—uh—nothing, ma'am! I mean—well—we were just interested."

Her faint smile returned.

"Well, it's a relief to talk to anyone who's genuinely interested. In fact"—the smile faded—"I've been thinking of hiring a private detective myself. Just to have *someone* take this seriously."

"Well, *I* take it seriously, Mrs. Getzoff," said Wanda.

"Yeah!" said McGurk. "We all do. Right, men?"

We murmured our agreement.

Mrs. Getzoff looked a little scared.

"Oh—but—but you don't think something bad has happened, do you? I mean *really* bad?"

"Well, no," said McGurk. "I mean who knows until there's some real evidence? All I meant was that we don't think things like people disappearing should be brushed off as—uh—well—teenage goofing-off or—or—"

"Or 'domestic problems,' " said Mrs. Getzoff. "No . . ."

She looked like she might start crying again. Wanda wasn't looking any too happy, either.

The cuckoo in the clock whirred and yelled four times.

"Four o'clock already?" said McGurk, standing up. "I guess it's time we were going. Thanks for the milk and cookies, ma'am. . . ."

Mealy's house was only just around the corner, but when we got there, Mrs. Oates's car was already in the driveway.

McGurk shrugged. He didn't look half as disappointed as I'd expected.

"We'll just have to leave it until tomorrow, men," he said.

Back along East Olive, just before we split up outside Brains's house, McGurk said, partly to himself, partly to me,

"Something tells me this case has taken a whole new direction." He lowered his voice and kept an eye on Wanda, as she strode ahead. "A lot more serious than the weathervane caper itself."

"Oh?" I murmured. "Want to tell me about it?"

"No. Not yet. I have to go over it in my head. Every detail. Every scrap of information."

I don't think I've ever seen McGurk look so grave. In fact, the thought flashed through my mind, right then and there: Why, anyone would think we'd a *murder* case on our hands!

13 Trunky

As far as the case was concerned, Friday started calm and ended in a hurricane.

At school, neither Wanda nor Brains had any fresh news about the missing persons. McGurk seemed relieved.

"Now maybe we can get on with our routine investigations," he said. "I want you all to muster at HQ straight after school. We'll go over everything we've learned so far. Then we'll tackle Mealy. Head on!"

His eyes gleamed and his lips were set tight when he'd finished speaking. We all knew the signs. No one was more than a couple of minutes late.

By the time Willie and I got there, McGurk had already added the new developments to my timetable. Here it is, just as *he* had typed it—not *I*:

```
WED NIGHXT
    ed's car foxund in parking GaraGe.
    Cops not excited.

    MR. Getzoff makes phone call █(around
    '#8.30) and goes out saying he"ll be
    back laxter.  Not seen or heard from
    since.

tHURSDAY AFTERNOON
    McGurk Organization interview MRs.
Getzoff and discover facts about mr. G's
disappearxance.  █(See also additions
to Tue and Wed timetable.
```

McGurk was making those additions, in pen, when the others arrived. Squeezed in between the entries for Tuesday, he scribbled: *TUE. AFT.—Mr. Truswell makes inquiries at Getzoff house. Mr. G. tells him how he suspects Ed.*

At the end of the Tuesday evening entry, he noted that Mr. Getzoff had started feeling uneasy about mentioning Ed. And at the end of the Wednesday morning entry, he added, *Mr. G. hears of Ed's disappearance and becomes* very *depressed.*

"Okay," he said. "Now we're all up-to-date. So—"

There was a knock at the door.

It was Mr. Truswell again.

Again he wouldn't come right in—just stood with his back to the open door, looking down on us with his sharp little eyes.

"I won't keep you long, McGurk," he said.

"That's okay, sir," said McGurk.

I noticed he'd been careful to turn the timetable sheets over. I guess he didn't want a rival detective to see any mention of Mealy Oates.

The man was slightly flushed—a kind of dusky purple—and there was a livelier gleam in his button eyes than I'd seen before. For a moment, I wondered if he'd been drinking. Then I realized it was triumph.

"I've just had a tipoff," he said. "I thought maybe you might help."

"Oh? Uh—sure!"

McGurk gulped and forced a grin.

"It seems we were right," said Truswell. "It *was* a student prank. Kid by the name of Trunky. Any idea where he lives?"

The detective's eyes started flicking from face to

face. The name hadn't caused any reaction from most of us. But Wanda had gasped, and McGurk had sighed.

McGurk's was obviously a sigh of relief. Mealy was *his* prime suspect, and so long as the man hadn't gotten hold of *that* name, McGurk was happy.

But Wanda's gasp puzzled me. She was staring at the man with her mouth still open and her face turning redder and redder.

"I don't know of anyone called *that*," said Mc-Gurk. "Who told you this, sir?"

The man ignored him. He was staring at Wanda.

"You know a Trunky, little girl?" he asked.

Wanda's eyes were looking this way and that, like she was standing in the path of a charging bull and wondering which way to jump.

"Well—yes," she said, in a faint voice. "But—well—"

"Come on!" said the man, with a rasp. "I'll find out, anyway. And I guarantee he won't get in trouble with the law."

Wanda blinked.

"Well—I don't *know* where he lives. Not exactly. Not his address. All I know is he lives over in Johnsonville."

We were all staring at her. Johnsonville is a fairly large-sized town about ten miles away.

"How come you know him then?" said the man. "Did he *use* to live here?"

Flick! Flick! Flick! Flick! Flick!

The little eyes had given each of the rest of us a quick checking glance. None of *us* could help him—that was obvious.

"No," said Wanda. "He's a friend of my brother's. They met in summer camp, a few years back."

"Hm! Johnsonville, huh? Looks like I still have

some more legwork. . . . Do you happen to know his other name, his surname?"

"Yes, sir," said Wanda. "Woods. Either Wood or Woods."

"Wood or Woods . . ." the man repeated, half to himself. "I see. . . ."

"I guess that's why he was nicknamed Trunky," said Wanda.

The man nodded.

"Yes. Sure." He looked at McGurk. "Well, that's private investigation work, son. Now I have to wear out shoe leather looking all over Johnsonville for a kid called Trunky Woods. Or Wood. Believe me, there's better ways to earn a living!"

"Why don't you—?" McGurk began, but the man was already on his way.

McGurk shrugged.

"I was going to suggest he look through the phone book, but I guess he knows all about that," he said. "Anyway, who is this guy Trunky? *Is* he the kind who might have pulled off a caper like this?"

Wanda shook her head. She went over to the door and peered out. Then she came back. Her face was very pale now.

"There's no such person," she said. "I made it up."

"Huh?"

"The name Trunky. I invented it."

"What *is* this?" McGurk growled. "He mentioned it first. So how could you—?"

"Trunky was an imaginary being. When—when I was very little." Wanda's lips were quivering slightly. "I had this imaginary friend. A pygmy elephant. He went with me everywhere. Except nights. Then—then he slept up in a tree. I called him Trunky."

"But—"

McGurk was staring at her as if she'd gone crazy. She blinked.

"Don't you *see*?" she cried. "There was only one other person in the whole world who ever knew about Trunky!"

"Hey!" gasped McGurk. "You don't mean—"

"Yes, I do!" said Wanda. "My brother Ed!"

14 A Bad Apple?

There was dead silence. Willie broke it.

"Wow!" he gasped.

McGurk looked shocked.

"It means he must have been talking to Ed!" he murmured.

"Yes," said Brains. "But where? And when? Ed's been gone more than two days!"

"It must have been since Wednesday afternoon," said Mari. "The man did not mention Trunky *then*."

"Sure!" said Wanda. "But whenever and wherever, why should Ed tell him *that* name?"

"To put him on a false scent?" I suggested.

"But why Trunky?" said Wanda. "Why not some other made-up name?"

"Yeah!" McGurk looked troubled. "You know what I'm beginning to think? I think—"

"I think it was meant for *us*!" said Wanda. "I think Ed was counting on the man asking us about Trunky. And—and on me realizing what has happened."

"What *has* happened?" said Willie.

"I—" Wanda began. Her lower lip trembled.

"What's happened, Officer Sandowsky," said McGurk, "what it looks like—is that he's got Ed— uh—holed up someplace."

"Holed up?" gasped Brains.

McGurk glanced cautiously at Wanda.

"Well—holding him prisoner."

"What?" said Brains. "But he's only a *private* detective!"

"I know," said McGurk. "But finding that weathervane—whichever one it is—must mean a lot to him. I think he's taken the law into his own hands."

"He must be crazy!" said Willie. "Mad!"

Wanda closed her eyes.

"Oh—but—but—" she stammered.

It must have been tough on her, listening to all this.

"Mad—maybe," said McGurk. "More likely just plain bad. A bad apple. There's one in every barrel. Even in the regular police."

Willie gaped.

"Like taking bribes?"

"Not just that," said McGurk. "But cutting corners. Forcing confessions. That kind of thing."

Wanda took a deep breath.

"Well, I'm going to the regular police right now! He might be hurting Ed. He—"

"Hold it a minute, Officer Grieg!"

Wanda paused at the door.

"But—"

"It seems to me that Ed must be in pretty good shape, thinking up a ruse like that," said McGurk. "And since you were smart enough to follow up with the Johnsonville story, the guy'll be busy for the next two or three hours."

"Sure!" said Wanda. "But I can't just—"

"You can't just go rushing off to the cops unprepared!" said McGurk. "All I'm asking is that you take a few minutes to *get* prepared. . . . Officer Yoshimura, go see if his car's still there. He might be making notes. So—without letting him spot *you*—see if you can get the license-plate number, make, and model of the car."

"Yes, Chief McGurk!" said Mari, already on her way.

Brains cleared his throat.

"I—uh—didn't get the number—but on Wednesday I noticed it was a Dodge Aries. Four-door sedan, silver gray, with Connecticut plates."

"I didn't get the number, either," I said. "But I remember the letters. *APM.*"

"You sure?" said McGurk.

"Yes," I said. "Because it was a mixture of AM and PM."

Mari came in, shaking her head. McGurk turned to Brains and me.

"Nice work, you two! *Those* details should help the cops. Write them down, Officer Rockaway, so that Officer Grieg can pass them on."

Wanda was looking better already.

"I wish we knew where he was staying, though," she said, as I jotted down the details.

"We do have a phone number," I said. "It's probably a motel, seeing how he's a stranger."

"Yeah!" said McGurk. "Put that down, too, Officer Rockaway. The cops should be able to trace it."

I wrote it down on the same sheet as the car details.

"There you go!" I said.

"Thanks!" Wanda snatched at it.

"One more minute!" said McGurk. His freckles were bunched in a thoughtful frown. "It should be

easy enough for *us* to find out which motel." He
opened the interior door. "Officer Grieg, why don't
you slip upstairs now and call that number? It's okay.
Mom's out shopping."

Wanda was already on her way.

"And whoever answers," McGurk called after her,
"tell them it was a wrong number. But listen carefully to what they say. Then you'll have something
else to tell the cops."

Quietly closing the door, he turned to Mari.

"Listen, Officer Yoshimura!" he said. "I want you to go with her. Now—try not to let her hear you or she might flip—but give the cops a warning—"

He opened the door a crack, listening.

"Yes, Chief McGurk? A *warning*?"

"Yes," he whispered. "Tell them the guy's probably armed and dangerous. Got that? . . . And tell them he's probably killed one person already. Tell them I'll be along as soon as possible to explain, but—Oh, hi, Officer Grieg! Any luck?"

Wanda shook her head as she came back into the room.

"Not really. It must be a private house or apartment. I let it ring forty times, but no one answered."

"Huh!" grunted McGurk. "Anyway, get moving. Officer Yoshimura is going with you."

"Good!" Wanda gave Mari a grateful glance. "But what about you others?"

"We'll be along!" McGurk said grimly. "But first we've got to dig up some more information—something that'll really clinch it. . . . Now *move*, Officer Grieg! You're wasting time!"

15 The Sign of the Trident

When Wanda and Mari had gone, McGurk turned.

"Right, men! Mealy's."

He didn't say much else on the way except: "We've just got to get hold of that weathervane!"

"Which weathervane?" I asked. "I thought we were looking for the complete stash."

"Right now," grunted McGurk, "there's only one that's really important. The Getzoff submarine."

"But why?" said Willie.

"Because something tells me that that's the one Truswell really wants. And when the cops see it, they'll be sure to take it seriously."

We turned into the Oates driveway. Mealy's car was out there.

"Hey," said Willie, as McGurk headed straight

for the backyard. "Aren't you going to ring the bell? He may be inside."

"I don't care," said McGurk. "We haven't time to waste arguing. That stash has to be someplace out here."

"Maybe he's taken it somewhere else by now," I said.

McGurk scowled.

"He wouldn't dare! He'd never risk being caught with it in his car."

"Everything *looks* the same," Brains said. "The strip's still the same size. The fork's still stuck in the same place." He made an impatient clucking noise. "Those bags of leaves are still—" He broke off. "Uh—sorry, McGurk!"

McGurk was staring at him, a crazy glint in his eyes.

"No—no, Officer Bellingham," he said. "Go on! Tell us again what you said about them."

"Well—uh—they *are* a fire hazard. And—"

McGurk had plucked the fork out of the ground.

"Go on," he said. "Don't stop, Officer Bellingham!"

Brains took a step back.

"Uh—*hey*—McGurk! Take it easy! I—"

"It's okay, Officer Bellingham!" McGurk was wearing a strange, tight smile. "I owe you an apology. Just go on—about the fire hazard and what you said about Mrs. Oates."

"Well, it's true!" bleated Brains. "She just doesn't look the type of person to use bags of leaves for insulation."

"No," said McGurk. "But she leaves all the garden stuff to Mealy, right? So—" McGurk had started to jab the line of bags by the fence, sticking the fork into them viciously. "So where else"—stab!—"bet-

ter"—stab!—"than using these bags"—stab!—"as a temporary hiding place—"

Clink!

"Right?" yelled McGurk, pouncing on the bag that had clinked.

"Hey!" came a voice, as McGurk began tearing at the plastic.

It was Mealy, hollering from somewhere inside the house. McGurk took no notice. He was busy pulling weathervanes out from the leaves—a rooster (which he tossed aside), a leaping stag (tossed aside), a soaring eagle. . . .

McGurk glared up at us.

"Come on, men! Grab a bag each and start looking!"

Brains was already slashing one open with his Swiss Army knife.

"There's some more here!" he gasped.

Willie and I tore open our bags. Willie tugged out a flying goose. My bag was just leaves. I grabbed another.

"I've got it!"

We all turned at Brains's shout. It was his own weathervane—the magnifying glass, looking rather crumpled.

"Never mind that now!" snapped McGurk. "Keep looking for the submarine!"

He was bending over his second bag just as Mealy came up to us.

The unmasked perpetrator looked pale and alarmed.

"Hey," he mumbled, "please! I—I was going to take them back."

McGurk sighed as he straightened up. I think I know what was eating him. Normally, he would have *reveled* in this moment—telling the guy we'd caught red-handed that the game was up, and so on.

But McGurk knows when to put first things first.

"Sure, you were going to take them back, Kevin," he said, mildly. "So just tell us which bags have weathervanes in them and help save time."

Mealy frowned.

"But—are you going to tell the police?"

"No," said McGurk. "*You* are. But the weathervane caper is penny-ante stuff. So if you cooperate, I'm sure the cops'll go easy on you."

He pulled out another rooster and tossed it onto the growing pile.

"I don't understand," said Mealy.

McGurk frowned.

"Listen! One of those weathervanes—the Getzoff submarine—was more valuable than anyone dreamed of. It's probably made of solid gold or platinum. It—"

"McGurk!" I cried.

I held up the weathervane I'd just pulled out. It was a peculiar stubby shape for a submarine, but Brains took one glance and said, "Yes. That's it!"

It didn't look like gold to *me*. Just a dull greeny gray tarnished metal. McGurk's face fell.

"Officer Bellingham," he said, "check it. *Could* it be gold? Or—"

"Soon see," murmured Brains, taking it from me and scratching it with his knife. Then: "No. No way. That's plain old copper, crusted over with verdigris."

"Let *me* see!" muttered McGurk, grabbing it.

He looked terribly disappointed.

Then his eyes narrowed.

"Here's the engraving, anyway," he murmured. "Hm! . . . Looks a mighty long catalog number . . . 'APC'—I guess those are the store owner's initials. . . ."

We crowded around. McGurk had wet his finger and rubbed it over the inscription. He was right. It *was* long—three lines of small letters and figures and other symbols. Here's the copy he had me make:

Yes, I know. It doesn't help much, presented like that. But, for reasons that will soon become clear, that's the only way I've been allowed to show it.

Willie pointed to the symbol at the start of the second line.

"Looks like a gardening fork."

"That isn't a gardening fork," I said. "It's one of those spears that King Neptune is supposed to have toted around. A trident."

"Hey!" yelled Brains. "Trident! Yeah! The *latest* nuclear subs are in the Trident class. Eight are already in service and number nine is still being built—I think." He stared at the engraving in sudden awe. "At Groton," he whispered. "Near Mystic. Oh, boy!"

McGurk's eyes lighted up.

"Yeah! And this could be a code giving some kind of information about it. Something the store owner wanted to pass on in case he got killed!"

"Who by?" said Willie, looking around nervously.

"By the guy or guys closing in on him," said McGurk. "The afternoon the Getzoffs bought this."

"Getzoffs?" said Mealy, plucking his mustache.

"Yeah!" growled McGurk, gazing into space, visualizing, figuring, testing.

"But *he's* disappeared, too!" said Mealy. "Mr. Getzoff!"

"We know," said McGurk, grimly. "And why? Because of what he said on TV is why. It must have caught the attention of those killers—that killer—whichever. It looks to me like some kind of spy deal!"

"Hey, McGurk!" I said. "You think Truswell is one of them?"

"Yeah. I also think that when he came making his inquiries it stirred something in the back of Mr. Getzoff's mind—reminding him of the guy the store owner locked the door against, that afternoon." McGurk was still staring into space. "So when Mr. Getzoff called him up on Wednesday night—" He took a deep breath. "Anyway, that's why we have to get this weathervane to the cops as soon as possible. Come on, men!"

"Wait!" yelped Mealy.

McGurk turned.

"Look, I *told* you, Mealy! This is *far* more important than your dumb caper. That guy—that killer—is holding Ed Grieg a prisoner, and—"

"I believe you!" said Mealy. "I was only asking you to wait while I got the car started. I'll drive you to the police station *myself*, for pete's sake!"

16 Lieutenant Kaspar Thinks Again

Down at the police station, Wanda and Mari had been having a hard time. When we got there— leaving Mealy waiting in the parking lot—Wanda was looking ready to explode. Across the desk, the sergeant was staring thoughtfully at his blotter while Lieutenant Kaspar did the talking, his face a bright shiny pink, his eyes as blue as gas jets. He winced slightly when he saw McGurk, but went on speaking to Wanda.

"Listen. We've called your mother and she'll be here any minute. You can't expect us to go steaming into Johnsonville just on your say-so. Not with a story like that." He turned to McGurk and snorted. "Armed and dangerous! . . . Well?"

"I don't know why you wouldn't believe us, sir," said McGurk. "After all, we've helped you before. But anyway—the guy *is* dangerous. This proves it."

He took the submarine from under his coat and placed it on the desk.

The two men were electrified.

"Where'd you get that?" said the lieutenant.

"From the same stash where all the other missing weathervanes are," said McGurk.

"Where?" said the sergeant.

"We've also traced the perpetrator," said Mc-Gurk, still addressing the lieutenant. "And it isn't Ed Grieg. *He's* probably a prisoner. . . . Did you tell them, Officer Grieg?"

Wanda nodded. Lieutenant Kaspar growled.

"I'm asking you, McGurk, *right now*, to say where you found them!"

"Yes, sir. In a garbage bag. But that isn't important." McGurk pointed to the inscription. "You know what this refers to? Details about the latest Trident submarine—the ninth."

The lieutenant's mouth had opened wide. But now it closed with a snap as he stared at the inscription.

McGurk went on talking fast, telling him all we'd

learned about the Getzoffs and the store owner, plus the links between Truswell's arriving on the scene, the TV broadcasts, and the two disappearances. McGurk was just starting on Mari's suspicions regarding the man's accent when there was another interruption.

Mrs. Grieg—her eyes glinting behind her glasses.

"What's going on?" she demanded, marching up to the desk. "Have you found my son?" She turned. "Wanda, what *is* all this?"

The lieutenant answered. He looked very serious now.

"We think we have a strong lead, ma'am." He flashed McGurk a look of acknowledgment. "But if you'll just excuse me, I have an urgent phone call to make. . . . I'll take it in my office, sergeant," he said, as he hurried away with the weathervane.

We found out later that the call was to the FBI. It took less than five minutes, but when he returned he seemed galvanized.

"I'd like you all to wait in the room over there," he said.

"But—"

"If we're to get your son back to you unharmed, we have work to do, ma'am." He glanced at the page from my notebook that Wanda had handed in. "We'll get back to you shortly."

Well, everyone knows what happened next. Or as much of it as the FBI would disclose. *They* got into the act immediately—the description of the Getzoff submarine's inscription had seen to *that*! In fact, this had been the first break in a case they'd had on their files for two years—a case that I am *still* not allowed to give many details of.

But first things first.

Thanks to our information, the man who *called* himself Truswell was picked up outside the house of someone named Woods, with the phone book in which he'd been checking off addresses.

He was amazed, according to Patrolman Cassidy, who told us about it afterward. Amazed but remarkably cool.

"I guess he knew right away it was no good resisting or even trying to bluff his way out," our friend explained. "He was a real professional. They say he's a top-ranking officer back in his own country and he'd already done a couple of successful tours in England and New Zealand."

So he took the police and agents straight to the isolated vacation home he'd been using on the outskirts of town—one of several that his employers maintained in various parts of the state, supposedly for investment, but really for just such purposes as this. And there they found Ed and Mr. Getzoff in separate rooms, tied to beds, with their mouths taped—very uncomfortable but otherwise unharmed.

"We wondered at first why he hadn't killed Mr. Getzoff, but the FBI guys weren't surprised," said Mr. Cassidy. "They said we were thinking too much like cops, and this guy was no ordinary criminal."

"What do you mean?" said McGurk, obviously wondering how it was possible for any law enforcement agent to think *too* much like a cop.

"Well, number one—he wanted Ed to give him information about the perpetrator, so he could get his hands on that sub. Right? So, number two— until that happened, he had to keep Mr. Getzoff out of the way in case he remembered *too* much about that afternoon in the weathervane store and blew the whistle on him."

"But supposing he *had* got hold of the weathervane?" Wanda asked. "Would he—would he have killed them *then?*"

Mr. Cassidy shrugged.

"The FBI guys said probably not. All he wanted was to get out of the country with that information. If he got caught—too bad. He was prepared to be handed out a life sentence, if necessary, knowing that sooner or later a trade-off might be arranged. In exchange for one of *our* guys *they*'d caught.

But"—here the cop looked very fierce—"if he murdered an innocent private citizen, no *way* would he ever be traded. He knew *that*, all right!"

"How about the store owner then?" said McGurk, looking equally fierce (*still* thinking like a cop, I guess). "Wasn't he an innocent citizen? Murdered?"

Mr. Cassidy shook his head.

"Well, for one thing, that would be impossible to prove now. It *was* a car crash, you know. Whether he was forced off the road and into the river, or whether he just panicked while trying to shake off whoever was chasing him—who's to say?"

It was Mari who spotted that Mr. Cassidy hadn't fully answered McGurk's question.

"Was *he* an agent?" she asked.

"Not a professional one, no. Just someone who'd once worked at the submarine plant and was prepared to sell what he knew to the highest bidder. A traitor. But he'd had the sense to hide the plans or whatever he'd stolen someplace away from his store. The inscription gave exact details of that location—where he'd also stashed information about the guys he'd been dealing with. Including—uh—Truswell. The inscription was in some kind of code, but a very simple amateur one. So no wonder Truswell was so keen to get hold of it!"

"What country *did* he come from?" Willie asked.

Mr. Cassidy refused to answer.

"I've already told you more than enough," he said, "because—well—I think you *deserve* that much."

He was able to tell us about Mealy, though.

There would definitely be no charges against him: (a) because of his cooperation (stoutly vouched for by McGurk); (b) because it *was* just a student prank; and (c) the other agencies wanted as much of the matter as possible kept out of the news.

"In fact, the lieutenant is relieved," said Mr. Cassidy. "It wasn't *his* idea to make such a big thing out of the caper in the first place."

At first, McGurk was bitterly disappointed by all this secrecy. After all, this had been his big dream come true—stumbling across a real live enemy agent. And, in McGurk's view, the only way a case like that should end would have been for him to be called to Washington for milk and cookies in the Oval Office. Plus a Medal of Honor.

But he soon began to enjoy the very secrecy that had torpedoed such a dream-ending.

I mean he just wasn't *allowed* to pin up one of his usual boastful claims at the bottom of the Organization notice, like the one that said BANK ROBBERS BUSTED. In this case, he'd dearly have loved to put SPY RINGS SMASHED or AGENTS UNCOVERED.

"But there *is* something that wouldn't give secrets

away," he said finally, with a gleam in his eyes. "Something that would still say *something* about the case. Also, it'll be a reminder how a good detective should always be alert when something doesn't seem to fit. Like Officer Bellingham was when he sensed that people like Mrs. Oates don't use bags of leaves to insulate their houses. Like I was when I realized there had to be some other reason."

So you know what he had me type up for the notice? This:

```
 •                                          °
    FIRE HAZARDS DETECTED
 •                                          °
```

"Gee, thanks, McGurk!" said Brains, touched by the tribute.

Wanda, who'd been rooting for BROTHERS BAILED OUT, sniffed and said, "You're all heart, McGurk!"

But even she was pleased, really. . . .